The main lights in the room were set low and a large glitter ball revolved slowly from the ceiling, scattering the floor and walls with shards of silver light.

Max watched them dance over Cara's face in fascination, thinking that she looked like some kind of ethereal seraph with her bright eyes and pale, creamy skin against the glowing silver of her dress.

A strange elation twisted through him, triggering a lifting sensation throughout his whole body—as if all the things that had dragged him down in the past eighteen months were losing their weight and slowly drifting upward. The sadness he'd expected to keep on hitting him throughout the day was still notably absent, and instead there was a weird sense of rightness about being here.

With her.

Dear Reader,

I've always loved the story of *Beauty and the Beast*, so I was really interested in using the disfigured hero trope in a modern-day retelling. Only in this story I wanted our hero, Max, to have locked himself away from the outside world because of mental rather than physical scars.

And he's certainly been through some dark times when we first meet him.

But of course, in true fairy-tale style, the unexpected appearance of a woman—in this case our gutsy (but equally humbled) heroine Cara—forces him to work past his irascible nature and self-imposed solitude and reveal the kind, caring man that's been hiding underneath for the past eighteen months.

It was wonderful to see these two help each other overcome the trials they've been through as the story played out on the page, and regain their pride and sense of self, finally finding the peace they'd been desperately missing, to become whole again.

And it certainly is a roller-coaster ride for these two!

I hope you enjoy their journey, through all its exhilarating ups and painful downs, and find the same satisfaction that I did in their eventual liberation from shame and regret through self-healing and their binding love for each other.

With best wishes,

Christy

Unlocking Her Boss's Heart

—

Christy McKellen

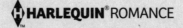
HARLEQUIN® ROMANCE

Recycling programs
for this product may
not exist in your area.

ISBN-13: 978-0-373-74371-1

Unlocking Her Boss's Heart

First North American Publication 2016

Copyright © 2016 by Christy McKellen

Printed in U.S.A.

HARLEQUIN®
www.Harlequin.com

Formerly a video and radio producer, **Christy McKellen** now spends her time writing fun, impassioned and emotive romance with an undercurrent of sensual tension. When she's not writing, she can be found enjoying life with her husband and three children, walking for pleasure and researching other people's deepest secrets and desires.

Christy loves to hear from readers. You can get ahold of her at christymckellen.com.

Books by Christy McKellen

Harlequin Romance

Unlocking Her Boss's Heart
is Christy McKellen's first Harlequin Romance title.

Harlequin Kiss

Holiday with a Stranger
Lessons in Rule-Breaking
Fired by Her Fling

Visit the Author Profile page
at Harlequin.com for more titles.

This one is for Babs and Phil,
the most generous, loving and supportive
parents in the world. You've seen me through
all my ups and downs (and there have been a
few) and always picked me up, dusted me off
and cheered me on.

I love you. I hope you know that.

CHAPTER ONE

CARA WINSTONE CLIMBED the smooth slate steps to the shiny black front door of the town house in South Kensington and tried hard not to be awed by its imposing elegance.

This place was exactly the sort of house she'd dreamed about living in during her naïve but hopeful youth. In her fantasies, the four-storey Victorian house would be alive with happy, mischievous children, whom she and her handsome husband would firmly but lovingly keep in line and laugh about in the evenings once they'd gone to bed. Each room would have a beautiful display of fresh seasonal flowers and light would pour in through the large picture windows, reflecting off the tasteful but comfortable furnishings.

Back in real life, her topsy-turvy one-bed flat in Islington was a million miles away from this grand goddess of a mansion.

Not that it was going to be her flat for much longer if she didn't make good on this opportunity today.

The triple espresso she'd had for breakfast lurched around in her stomach as she thought about how close she was to being evicted from the place she'd called home for the past six years by her greedy landlord. If she didn't find another job soon she was going to have to slink back to Cornwall, to the village that time forgot, and beg to share her parents' box room with the dogs until she got back on her feet.

She loved her parents dearly, but the thought of them all bumping elbows again in their tiny isolated house made her shudder. Especially after they'd been so excited when she'd called six months ago to tell them about landing her dream job as Executive Assistant to the CEO of one of the largest conglomerates in the country. Thanks to her mother's prodigious grapevine, word had quickly spread through both the family and her parents' local community and she'd been inundated with texts and emails of congratulations.

The thought of having to call them again

now and explain why she'd been forced to hand in her notice after only three months made her queasy with shame. She couldn't do it. Not after the sacrifices they'd made in order to pay for her expensive private education, so she'd have the opportunities they'd never had. No, she owed them more than that.

But, with any luck, she'd never be forced to have that humiliating conversation because this chance today could be the ideal opportunity to get her feet back under the table. If she could secure this job, she was sure that everything else would fall into place.

Shifting the folder that contained her CV and the glowing references she'd accumulated over the years under her arm, she pressed the shiny brass bell next to the door and waited to be greeted by the owner of the house.

And waited.

Tapping her foot, she smoothed down her hair again, then straightened the skirt of her best suit, wanting to look her most professional and together self when the door finally swung open.

Except that it didn't.

Perhaps the occupier hadn't heard her ring.

Fighting the urge to chew on the nails she'd

only just grown out, she rang again, for longer this time and was just about to give up and come back later when the door swung open to reveal a tall, shockingly handsome man with a long-limbed, powerful physique and the kind of self-possessed air that made her heart beat a little faster. His chocolate-brown hair looked as though it could do with a cut, but it fell across his forehead into his striking gold-shot hazel eyes in the most becoming manner. If she had to sum him up in one word it would be *dashing*—an old-fashioned-sounding term, but somehow it suited him down to the ground.

His disgruntled gaze dropped from her face to the folder under her arm.

'Yes?' he barked, his tone so fierce she took a pace backwards and nearly fell off the top step.

'Max Firebrace?' To her chagrin, her voice came out a little wobbly in the face of his unexpected hostility.

His frown deepened. 'I don't donate to charities at the door.'

Taking a deep breath, she plastered an assertive smile onto her face and said in her most patient voice, 'I'm not working for a charity. I'm here for the job.'

His antagonism seemed to crackle like a brooding lightning storm between them. 'What are you talking about? I'm not hiring for a job.'

Prickly heat rushed across her skin as she blinked at him in panicky confusion. 'Really? But my cousin Poppy said you needed a personal assistant because you're snowed under with work.'

He crossed his arms and shook his head as an expression of beleaguered understanding flashed across his face.

'I only told Poppy I'd look into hiring someone to get her off my back,' he said irritably.

She frowned at him in confusion, fighting the sinking feeling in her gut. 'So you don't need a PA?'

Closing his eyes, he rubbed a hand across his face and let out a short, sharp sigh. 'I'm very busy, yes, but I don't have time to even interview for a PA right now, let alone train them up, so if you'll excuse me—'

He made as if to shut the door, but before he could get it halfway closed she dashed forwards, throwing up both hands in a desperate attempt to stall him and dropping her folder onto the floor with a loud clatter. 'Wait! Please!'

A look of agitated surprise crossed his face at the cacophony, but at least he paused, then opened the door a precious few inches again.

Taking that as a sign from the gods of perseverance, Cara scooped up her folder from the floor, threw back her shoulders and launched into the sales pitch she'd been practising since Poppy's email had landed in her inbox last night, letting her know about this golden opportunity.

'I'm *very* good at what I do and I'm a quick learner—I have six years of experience as a PA so you won't need to show me much at all.' Her voice had taken on an embarrassing squeaky quality, but she soldiered on regardless.

'I'm excellent at working on my own initiative and I'm precise and thorough. You'll see when you hire me,' she said, forcing a confidence she didn't feel any more into her voice.

He continued to scowl at her, his hand still gripping the door as if he was seriously contemplating shutting it in her face, but she was not about to leave this doorstep without a fight. She'd had *enough* of feeling like a failure.

'Give me a chance to show you what I can do, free of charge, today, then if you like what you see I can start properly tomorrow.' Her forced smile was beginning to make her cheeks ache now.

His eyes narrowed as he appeared to consider her proposal.

After a few tense seconds of silence, where she thought her heart might beat its way out of her chest, he nodded towards the folder she was still clutching in her hand.

'Is that your CV?' he asked.

'Yes.' She handed it to him and watched with bated breath as he flipped through it.

'Okay,' he said finally, sighing hard and shoving the folder back towards her. 'Show me what you can do today, then if I'm satisfied I'll offer you a paid one-month trial period. After *that* I'll decide whether it's going to work out as a full-time position or not.'

'Done.' She stuck out a hand, which he looked at with a bemused expression, before enveloping it in his own large, warm one.

Relief, chased by an unnerving hot tingle,

rushed through her as he squeezed her fingers, causing every nerve-ending on her body to spring to life.

'You'd better come in,' he said, dropping the handshake and turning his broad back on her to disappear into the house.

Judging by his abrupt manner, it seemed she had her work cut out if she was going to impress him. Still, she was up for the challenge—even if the man did make her stomach flip in the most disconcerting way.

Shaking off her nerves, she hurried inside after him, closing the heavy door behind her and swivelling back just in time to see him march into a doorway at the end of the hall.

And what a hall. It had more square footage than her entire flat put together. The high, pale cream walls were lined with abstract works of art on real canvases, not clip-framed prints like she had at her place, and the colourful mosaic-tiled floor ran for what must have been a good fifty metres before it joined the bottom of a wide oak staircase which led up to a similarly grand stairwell, where soft light flooded in through a huge stained-glass window.

Stopping by a marble-topped hall table,

which, she noted, was sadly devoid of flowers, she took a deep calming breath before striding down the hallway to the room he'd vanished into.

Okay, she could do this. She could be impressive. Because she *was* impressive.

Right, Cara? *Right?*

The room she entered was just as spacious as the hall, but this time the walls were painted a soft duck-egg blue below the picture rail and a crisp, fresh white above it, which made the corniced ceiling feel as if it was a million miles above her and that she was very small indeed in comparison.

Max was standing in the middle of the polished parquet floor with a look of distracted impatience on his face. Despite her nerves, Cara couldn't help but be aware of how dauntingly charismatic he was. The man seemed to give off waves of pure sexual energy.

'My name's Cara, by the way,' she said, swallowing her apprehension and giving him a friendly smile.

He just nodded and held out a laptop. 'This is a spare. You can use it today. Once you've set it up, you can get started on scanning and filing those documents over there,' he said, pointing to a teetering pile of paper on a table by the window. 'There's the filing cabinet—' he swung his finger to point at it '—there's the scanner.' Another swing of his finger. 'The filing system should be self-explanatory,' he concluded with barely concealed agitation in his voice.

So he wasn't a people person then.

'Okay, thank you,' she said, taking the laptop from him and going to sit on a long, low sofa that was pushed up against the wall on the opposite side of the room to a large oak desk with a computer and huge monitor on top of it.

Tamping down on the nervous tension that had plagued her ever since she'd walked away from her last job, she booted up the laptop, opened the internet browser and set up her email account and a folder called 'Firebrace Management Solutions' in a remote file-saving app. Spotting a stack of business cards on the coffee table next to the sofa, she swiped one and programmed Max's mobile number into her phone, then added his email address to her contacts.

Throughout all this, he sat at his desk with his back to her, deeply absorbed in writing the document she must have stopped him from working on when she'd knocked on his door.

Okay. The first thing she was going to do was make them both a hot drink, then she'd make a start on the mountain of paperwork to be digitally backed up and filed.

Not wanting to speak up and disturb him with questions at this point, she decided to do a bit of investigative work. Placing the laptop carefully onto the sofa, she stood up and made for the door, intent on searching out the kitchen.

He didn't stir from his computer screen as she walked past him.

Well, if nothing else, at least this was going to be a very different experience to her last job. By the end of her time there she could barely move without feeling a set of judging eyes burning into her.

The kitchen was in the room directly opposite and she stood for a moment to survey the lie of it. There was a big glass-topped table in the middle with six chairs pushed in around it and an expanse of cream-coloured marble work surface, which ran the length of two sides of the room. The whole place was sleek and new-looking, with not a thing out of place.

Opening up the dishwasher, she peered inside and saw one mug and one cereal bowl sitting in the rack. *Hmm.* So it was just Max living here? Unless his partner was away at the moment. Glancing round, she scanned the place for photographs, but there weren't any, not even one stuck to the enormous American fridge. In fact, this place was so devoid of personalised knick-knacks it could have been a kitchen in a show home.

Lifting the mug out of the dishwasher, she checked it for remnants of his last drink, noting from the smell that it was coffee, no sugar, and from the colour that he took it without milk. There was a technical-looking coffee maker on the counter which flummoxed her for a moment or two, but she soon figured out how to set it up and went about finding coffee grounds in the sparsely filled fridge and making them both a drink, adding plenty of milk to hers.

Walking back into the room, she saw that Max hadn't budged a centimetre since she'd left and was still busy tapping away on the keyboard.

After placing his drink carefully onto the desk, which he acknowledged with a grunt, she took a look through the filing cabinet till she figured out which system he was using, then squared up to the mountain of paperwork on the sideboard, took a breath and dived in.

Well, she was certainly the most *determined* woman he'd met in a long time.

Max Firebrace watched Cara out of the corner of his eye as she manhandled the pile of documents over to the sofa and heard her put them down with a thump on the floor.

Glancing at the drink she'd brought him, he noticed she'd made him a black coffee without even asking what he wanted.

Huh. He wasn't expecting that. The PAs he'd had in the past had asked a lot of questions when they'd first started working with him, but Cara seemed content to use her initiative and just get on with things.

Perhaps this wasn't going to be as much of a trial as he'd assumed when he'd agreed to their bargain on the doorstep.

It was typical of Poppy to send someone over here without letting him know. His friend was a shrewd operator all right. She'd known he was blowing her off when he promised to get someone in to help him and had clearly taken it upon herself to make it happen anyway.

Irritation made his skin prickle.

He was busy, sure, but, as he'd told Poppy at the time, it wasn't anything he couldn't handle. He'd allow Cara to work her one-month trial period to placate his friend, but then he'd let her go. He wasn't ready to hire someone else full-time yet; there wasn't enough for her to do day-to-day, and he didn't need someone hanging around, distracting him.

Leaning back into the leather swivel chair that had practically become his home in the past few months, he rubbed the heels of his hands across his eyes before picking up the drink and taking a sip.

He'd been working more and more at the weekends now that his management consultancy was starting to grow some roots, and he was beginning to feel it. It had been a slog since he'd set up on his own, but he'd been glad of the distraction and it was finally starting to pay dividends. If things carried on in the same vein, at some point in the future he'd be in a position to rent an office, hire some employees and start expanding. *Then* he could relax a little and things would get back to a more even keel.

The thought buoyed him. After working for other people since graduating from university, he was enjoying having full control over who he worked for and when; it seemed to bring about a modicum of peace—something that had eluded him for the past eighteen months. Ever since Jemima had gone.

No, *died*.

He really needed to allow the word into his interior monologue now. No one else had wanted to say it at the time, so he'd become used to employing all the gentler euphemisms himself, but there was no point pretending it was anything else. She'd died, so suddenly and unexpectedly it had left him reeling for months, and he still wasn't used to living in this great big empty house without her. The house Jemima had inherited from her great-aunt. The home she'd wanted to fill with children—which he'd asked her to wait for—until *he* felt ready.

Pain twisted in his stomach as he thought about all that he'd lost—his beautiful, compassionate wife and their future family. Recently he'd been waking up at night in a cold sweat, reaching out to try and save a phantom child with Jemima's eyes from a fall, or a fire—the shock and anguish of it often staying with him for the rest of the following day.

No wonder he was tired.

A movement in the corner of his eye broke his train of thought and he turned to watch Cara as she opened up the filing cabinet to the right of him and began to deftly slide documents into the manila folders inside.

Now that he looked at her properly, he could see the family resemblance to Poppy. She had the same shiny coal-black hair as his friend, which cascaded over her slim shoulders, and a very short blunt-cut fringe above bright blue almond-shaped eyes.

She was pretty. Very pretty, in fact.

Not that he had any interest in her romantically. It was purely an observation.

Cara looked round and caught him watching her, her cheeks flushing in response to his scrutiny.

Feeling uncomfortable with the atmosphere he'd created by staring at her, he sat up straighter, crossing his arms and adopting a more businesslike posture. 'So, Cara, tell me about the last place you worked. Why did you leave?'

Her rosy cheeks seemed to pale under his direct gaze. Rocking back on her heels, she cleared her throat, her gaze skittering away from his to stare down at the papers in her hands, as if she was priming herself to give him an answer she thought he'd want to hear.

What was *that* about? The incongruity made him frown.

'Or were you fired?'

Her gaze snapped back to his. 'No, no, I left. At least, I opted for voluntary redundancy. The business I was working for took a big financial hit last year and, because I was the last in, it felt only right that I should be the first out. There were lots of people who worked there with families to support, whereas I'm only me—I mean I don't have anyone depending on me.'

Her voice had risen throughout that little monologue and the colour had returned to her cheeks to the point where she looked uncomfortably flushed. There was something not quite right about the way she'd delivered her answer, but he couldn't put his finger on what it was.

Perhaps she was just nervous? He knew he could come across as fierce sometimes, though usually only when someone did something to displease him.

He didn't suffer fools gladly.

But she'd been fine whilst persuading him to give her a shot at the PA job.

'That's it? You took voluntary redundancy?'

She nodded and gave him a smile that didn't quite reach her eyes. 'That's it.'

'So why come begging for this job? Surely, with your six years of experience, you could snap up a senior position in another blue-chip firm and earn a lot more money.'

Crossing her arms, she pulled her posture up straighter, as if preparing to face off with him. 'I wouldn't say I *begged* you for this job—'

He widened his eyes, taken aback by the defensiveness in her tone.

Noting this, she sank back into her former posture and swept a conciliatory hand towards him. '—but I take your point. To be honest, I've been looking for a change of scene from the corporate workplace and when Poppy mailed me about this opportunity it seemed to fit with exactly what I was looking for. I like the idea of working in a small, dedicated team and being an intrinsic part of the growth of a new business. Poppy says you're brilliant at what you do and I like working for brilliant people.' She flashed him another smile, this time with a lot more warmth in it.

He narrowed his eyes and gave her an approving nod. 'Okay. Good answer. You're an excellent ambassador for yourself and that's a skill I rate highly.'

Her eyes seemed to take on an odd shine in the bright mid-morning light, as if they'd welled up with tears.

Surely not.

Breaking eye contact, she looked down at the papers in her hand and blinked a couple of times, giving the floor a small nod. 'Well, that's good to hear.' When she looked back up, her eyes were clear again and the bravado in her expression made him wonder what was going on in her head.

Not that he should concern himself with such things.

An odd moment passed between them as their gazes caught and he became uncomfortably aware of the silence in the room. He'd been on his own in this house for longer than he wanted to think about, and having her here was evidently messing with his head. Which was exactly what he didn't need.

Cara looked away first, turning to open one of the lower filing cabinet drawers. After dropping the documents into it, she turned back to face him with a bright smile. 'Okay, well, it won't take me too much longer to finish this so I'll nip out in a bit and get us some lunch from the café a couple of streets away. When I walked past earlier there was an amazing smell of fresh bread wafting out of there, and they had a fantastic selection of deli meats and cheeses and some delicious-looking salads.'

Max's stomach rumbled as he pictured the scene she'd so artfully drawn in his mind. He was always too busy to go out and fetch lunch for himself, so ended up eating whatever he could forage from the kitchen, which usually wasn't much.

'Then, if you have a spare minute later on, you can give me access to your online diary,' Cara continued, not waiting for his response. 'I'll take a look through it and organise any transport and overnight stays you need booking.'

'Okay. That would be useful,' he said, giving her a nod. It would be great to have the small daily inconveniences taken care of so he could concentrate on getting this report knocked into shape today.

Hmm. Perhaps it would prove more advantageous than he'd thought to have her around for a while.

He'd have to make sure he fully reaped the benefit of her time here before letting her go.

CHAPTER TWO

SHE WAS A terrible liar.

The expression on Max's face had been sceptical at best when she'd reeled out the line about leaving her last job, but Cara thought she'd pulled it off. At least he hadn't told her to sling her hook.

Yet.

She got the impression he was the type of person who wouldn't tolerate any kind of emotional weakness—something she was particularly sensitive to after her last boyfriend, Ewan, left her three months ago because he was fed up with her 'moaning and mood swings'. So she was going to have to be careful not to let any more momentary wobbles show on her face. It was going to be happy, happy, joy, joy! from here on in.

After slipping the last document into the filing cabinet, taking care not to let him see how much her hands were still shaking, she grabbed her coat and bag and, after taking a great gulp of crisp city air into her lungs, went to the café to pick up some lunch for them both, leaving the door off the latch so she wouldn't have to disturb Max by ringing the bell on her return.

Inevitably, she bought a much bigger selection of deli wares than the two of them could possibly eat in one session, but she told herself that Max could finish off whatever remained for his supper. Judging by the emptiness of his cavernous fridge, he'd probably be glad of it later.

This made her wonder again about his personal situation. Poppy had told her very little in the email—which she'd sent in a rare five minutes off from her crazy-sounding filming schedule in the African desert. Cara didn't want to bother her cousin with those kinds of questions when she was so busy, so it was up to her to find out the answers herself. For purely professional reasons, of course. It would make her working life much easier if she knew whether she needed to take a partner's feelings into consideration when making bookings away from the office.

Surprisingly, Max didn't put up much resistance to being dragged away from his computer with the promise of lunch and came into the kitchen just as she'd finished laying out the last small pot of pimento-stuffed olives, which she hadn't been able to resist buying.

'Good timing,' she said as he sat down. 'That deli is incredible. I wasn't sure what you'd prefer so I got just about everything they had—hopefully, there'll be something you like—and there should be plenty left over for tomorrow, or this evening if you don't already have dinner plans.'

Good grief—could she jabber more?

Clearly, this had occurred to Max too because he raised his eyebrows, but didn't say a word.

Trying not to let his silence intimidate her, Cara passed him a plate, which he took with an abrupt nod of thanks, and she watched him load it up with food before tucking in.

'So, Max,' she said, taking a plate for herself and filling it with small triangular-cut sandwiches stuffed with soft cheese and prosciutto and a spoonful of fluffy couscous speckled with herbs and tiny pieces of red pepper. 'How do you know Poppy? She didn't tell me anything about you—other than that you're friends.'

He gave a small shrug. 'We met at university.'

Cara waited for him to elaborate.

He didn't. He just kept on eating.

Okay, so he wasn't the sort to offer up personal details about himself and liked to keep things super professional with colleagues, but perhaps she'd be able to get more out of him once they'd built up a rapport between them.

That was okay. It was early days yet. She could bide her time.

At least she had some company for lunch, even if he wasn't interested in talking much. She'd spent all her lunchtimes at her last place of work alone, either sitting in the local park or eating a sandwich at her desk, forcing the food past her constricted throat, trying not to care about being excluded from the raucous group of PAs who regularly lunched together. The Cobra Clique, she'd called them in her head.

Not to their faces.

Never to their faces.

Because, after making the mistake of assuming she'd be welcomed into their group

when she'd first started working there—
still riding on a wave of pride and excitement about landing such a coveted job—she'd
soon realised that she'd stepped right into the
middle of a viper's nest. Especially after the
backlash began to snap its tail a couple of
days into her first week.

Fighting the roll of nausea that always assaulted her when she thought about it, she
took a large bite of sandwich and chewed
hard, forcing herself to swallow, determined
not to let what had happened bother her any
more. They'd won and she was not going to
let them keep on winning.

'It's a beautiful house you have, Max,' she
said, to distract herself from the memories
still determinedly circling her head. 'Have
you been here long?'

His gaze shot to hers and she was alarmed
to see him frown. 'Three years,' he said, with
a clip of finality to his voice, as if wanting
to make it clear he didn't want to discuss the
subject any more.

Okay then.

From the atmosphere that now hummed between them, you'd have thought she'd asked
him how much cold hard cash he'd laid down

for the place. Perhaps people did ask him that regularly and he was fed up with answering it. Or maybe he thought she'd ask for a bigger wage if she thought he was loaded.

Whatever the reason, his frostiness had now totally destroyed her appetite, so she was pushing the couscous around her plate when Max stood up, making her jump in her seat.

'Let me know how much I owe you for lunch and I'll get it out of petty cash before you leave,' he said, turning abruptly on the spot and heading over to the dishwasher to load his empty plate into it.

His movements were jerky and fast, as if he was really irritated about something now.

It couldn't be her, could it?

No.

Could it?

He must just be keen to get back to work.

As soon as he left the room, she let out the breath she'd been holding, feeling the tension in her neck muscles release a little.

The words *frying pan* and *fire* flitted through her head, but she dismissed them. If he was a friend of Poppy's he couldn't be that bad. She must have just caught him on a bad day. And, as her friend Sarah had pointed out after she'd cried on her shoulder about making a mess of her recent job interviews, she was bound to be prone to paranoia after her last experience.

Once she'd cleared up in the kitchen, Cara got straight back to work, using the link Max gave her to log in to his online diary and work through his travel requirements for the next month. His former ire seemed to have abated somewhat and their interaction from that point onwards was more relaxed, but still very professional. Blessedly, concentrating on the work soothed her and the headache that had started at the end of lunch began to lift as she worked methodically through her tasks.

Mid-afternoon, Max broke off from writing his document for a couple of minutes to outline some research he wanted her to do on a few businesses he was considering targeting. To her frustration, she had to throw every molecule of energy into making scrupulous notes in order to keep focused on the task in hand and not on the way Max's masculine scent made her senses reel and her skin heat with awareness every time he leaned closer to point something out on the computer they were huddled around.

That was something she was going to have to conquer if they continued to work together, which hopefully they would. She definitely couldn't afford a crush on her boss to get in the way of her recuperating future.

After finally being released from the duress of his unnerving presence, she spent the remainder of the day happily surfing the internet and collating the information into a handy crib sheet for him, revelling in the relief of getting back into a mindset she'd taken for granted until about six months ago, before her whole working life had been turned inside out.

At five-thirty she both printed out the document and emailed it to him, then gathered up her coat and bag, feeling as though she'd done her first good day's work in a long time.

Approaching his desk, she cleared her throat and laid the printout onto it, trying not to stare at the way his muscles moved beneath his slim-fitting shirt while she waited for him to finish what he was typing. Tearing her eyes away from his broad back, she took the opportunity to look at his hands instead, noting with a strange satisfaction that he wasn't wearing a wedding ring on his long, strong-looking fingers.

Okay, not married then. But surely he must have a girlfriend. She couldn't imagine someone as attractive as Max being single.

He stopped typing and swivelled round in his chair to face her, startling her out of her musings and triggering a strange throb, low in her body.

'You've done well today; I'm impressed,' he said, giving her a slow nod.

She couldn't stop her mouth from springing up into a full-on grin. It had been a long while since she'd been complimented on her work and it felt ridiculously good.

'Thank you—I've really enjoyed it.'

His raised eyebrow told her she'd been a bit over-effusive with that statement, but he unfolded his arms and dipped his head thoughtfully.

'If you're still interested, I'm willing to go ahead with the one-month trial.'

Her squeak of delight made him blink. 'I can't promise there'll be a full-time job at the end of it, though,' he added quickly.

She nodded. 'Okay, I understand.' She'd

just have to make sure she'd made herself indispensable by the end of the month.

He then named a weekly wage that made her heart leap with excitement. With money like that she could afford to stay in London and keep on renting her flat.

'I'll see you here at nine tomorrow then,' he concluded, turning back to his computer screen.

'Great. Nine o'clock tomorrow,' she repeated, smiling at the back of his head and retreating out of the room.

She floated out of the house on a cloud of joy, desperate to get home so she could phone her landlord and tell him she was going to be able to make next month's rent so he didn't need to find a new tenant for her flat.

It was all going to be okay now; she could feel it.

Back in her flat, she dialled her landlord's number and he answered with a brusque, 'Yes.'

'Dominic—it's Cara Winstone. I'm calling with good news. I've just started at a new job so I'll be able to renew my lease on your property in Islington.'

There was a silence at the end of the phone,

followed by a long sigh. 'Sorry, Cara, but I've already promised my nephew he can move in at the end of the week. I got the impression you wouldn't be able to afford the rent any more and I've kept it pitifully low for the last couple of years already. I can't afford to sub you any more.'

Fear and anger made her stomach sink and a suffocating heat race over her skin as she fully took in what he'd just said. He was such a liar. He'd been hiking the rent up year on year until she'd felt as if she was being totally fleeced, but she hadn't wanted the hassle of moving out of her comfortable little flat so she'd sucked it up. Until she wasn't able to any more.

'Can't you tell your nephew that your current tenant has changed her mind?' Even as she said it she knew what his answer was going to be.

'No. I can't. You had your chance to renew. I couldn't wait any longer and my nephew was having trouble finding somewhere suitable to live. It's a cut-throat rental market in London at the moment.'

That was something she was about to find out herself, she felt sure of it.

'Do you have anywhere else available to

rent at the moment?' she asked, desperately grasping for some glimmer of a solution.

'No. Sorry.'

He didn't sound sorry, she noted with another sting of anger.

'You've got till the end of the week, then I want you out,' he continued. 'Make sure the place is in a good state when you leave or I'll have to withhold your damage deposit.' And, with that, he put the phone down on her.

It took a few minutes of hanging her head between her knees for the dizziness to abate and for her erratic heartbeat to return to normal.

Okay, this was just a setback. She could handle it.

Just because it would be hard to find a decent flat to rent in London at short notice didn't mean she wouldn't find somewhere else. She'd have to be proactive though and make sure to put all her feelers out, then respond quickly to any leads.

That could prove tricky now that she was working so closely with Max and she was going to have to be very careful not to mess up on the job, because it looked as though she was going to need things to work out there more than ever now.

* * *

The rest of the week flew by for Max, with Cara turning up exactly when she said she would and working diligently and efficiently through the tasks he gave her.

Whilst it was useful having her around to take care of some of the more mundane jobs that he'd been ignoring for far too long, he also found her presence was disrupting his ability to lose himself in his work, which he'd come to rely on in order to get through the fiercely busy days.

She was just so *jolly* all the time.

And she was making the place smell different. Every morning when he came downstairs for his breakfast he noticed her light floral perfume in the air. It was as though she was beginning to permeate the walls of his house and even the furniture with her scent.

It made him uncomfortable.

He knew he'd been rude during their first lunch together when Cara had asked him about the house and that he'd been unforthcoming about anything of a personal nature ever since—preferring to spend his lunchtimes in companionable silence—but he was concerned that any questions about himself would inevitably lead on to him having to talk about Jemima.

Work was supposed to be sanctuary from thinking about what had happened and he really didn't want to discuss it with Cara.

He also didn't want them to become too sociable because it would only make it harder for him to let her go after the promised month of employment.

Clearly she was very good at her job, so he had no concerns about her finding another position quickly after her time was up, but it might still prove awkward when it came down to saying no to full-time employment if they were on friendly terms. He suspected Cara's story about taking voluntary redundancy wasn't entirely based on truth and that she and Poppy had cooked up the story to play on his sympathy in order to get him to agree to take her on. While he was fine with allowing his errant friend to push him into a temporary arrangement to appease her mollycoddling nature, he wasn't going to allow her to bully him into keeping Cara on full-time.

He didn't need her.

After waking late on Friday morning and having to let an ebullient Cara in whilst still not yet ready to face the day, he had to rush his shower and hustle down to the kitchen with a pounding headache from not sleeping well the night before. Opening the fridge, he found that Cara had stocked it with all sorts of alien-looking food—things he would never have picked out himself. He knew he was bad at getting round to food shopping, but Cara's choices were clearly suggesting he wasn't looking after himself properly. There were superfoods galore in there.

He slammed the fridge door shut in disgust.

The damn woman was taking over the place.

Cara was in the hallway when he came out of the kitchen a few minutes later with a cup of coffee so strong he could have stood his spoon up in it. She waved a cheery hello, then gestured to a vase of brightly coloured flowers that she'd put onto the hall table, giving him a jaunty smile as if to say, *That's better, right?* which really set his teeth on edge. How was it possible for her to be so damn happy all the time? Did the woman live with her head permanently in the clouds?

They'd never had fresh flowers in the house when Jemima was alive because she'd suffered with bad hay fever from the pollen, and he was just about to tell Cara that when he caught himself and clamped his mouth shut. It wasn't a discussion he wanted to have this morning, with a head that felt as if it was about to explode. The very last thing he needed right now was Cara's fervent pity.

'I thought it would be nice to have a bit of colour in here,' she said brightly, oblivious to his displeasure. 'I walked past the most amazing florist's on my way over here and I just couldn't resist popping in. Flowers are so good for lifting your mood.'

'That's fine,' he said through gritted teeth, hoping she wasn't going to be this chipper all day. He didn't think his head could stand it.

'I'll just grab myself a cup of tea, then I'll be in,' she said.

Only managing to summon a grunt in response, he walked into the morning room that he'd turned into an office. He'd chosen it because it was away from the distractions of the street and in the odd moment of pause he found that staring out into the neatly laid garden soothed him. There was a particular brightly coloured bird that came back day after day and hopped about on the lawn, looking for worms, which captivated him. It wasn't there today, though.

After going through his ever-growing inbox and dealing with the quick and easy things, he opened up his diary to check what was going on that day. He had a conference call starting in ten minutes that would probably last till lunchtime, which meant he'd need to brief Cara now about what he wanted her to get on with.

Where was she, anyway?

She'd only been going to make herself a hot drink. Surely she must have done that by now?

Getting up from his chair with a sigh of irritation, he walked through to the kitchen to find her. The last thing he needed was to have to chase his PA down. It was going to be a demanding day which required some intense concentration and he needed her to be on the ball and ready to knuckle down.

She was leaning against the table with her back to the door when he walked into the kitchen, her head cocked to one side as if she was fascinated by something on the other side of the room.

He frowned at her back, wondering what

in the heck could be so absorbing, until she spoke in a hushed tone and he realised she was on the phone.

'I don't know whether I'll be able to get away at lunchtime. I have to fetch my boss's lunch and there's a ton of other stuff I have to wade through. His systems are a mess. Unfortunately, Max isn't the type you can ask for a favour either; he's not exactly approachable. I could make it over for about six o'clock, though,' she muttered into the phone.

The hairs rose on the back of his neck. She was making arrangements to see her friends on his time?

He cleared his throat loudly, acutely aware of the rough harshness of his tone in the quiet of the room.

Spinning around at the noise, Cara gave him a look of horror, plainly embarrassed to be caught out.

Definitely a personal call then.

Frustration rattled through him, heating his blood. How could he have been so gullible as to think it would be easy having her as an employee? Apparently she was going to be just as hard work to manage as all the other PAs he'd had.

'Are you sure you took redundancy at your last place? Or did they let you go for taking liberties on the job?' he said, unable to keep the angry disappointment out of his voice.

She swallowed hard and he found his gaze drawn to the long column of her throat, its smooth elegance distracting him for a second. Shaking off his momentary befuddlement, he snapped his gaze back to hers, annoyed with himself for losing concentration.

'I do not expect behaviour like this from someone with six years of experience as a personal assistant. This isn't the canteen where you waste time gossiping with your mates instead of doing the job you're being paid to do. Things like this make you look stupid and amateurish.'

She nodded jerkily but didn't say anything as her cheeks flushed with colour and a tight little frown appeared in the centre of her fore-head.

Fighting a twist of unease, he took another step forwards and pointed a finger at her. 'You do not take personal phone calls on my time. Is that understood? Otherwise, you and I are going to have a problem, and problems are the last thing I need right now. I took a chance on you because you came recommended by Poppy. Do not make a fool out of my friend. Or out of me.'

'I'm sorry—it won't ever happen again. I promise,' she said, her voice barely above a whisper.

The look in her eyes disturbed him. It was such a change from her usual cheery countenance that it sat uncomfortably with him. In fact, to witness her reaction you'd have thought he'd just slapped her around the face, not given her a dressing-down.

'See that it doesn't,' he concluded with a curt nod, an unnerving throb beginning to beat in his throat.

As he walked back into his office, he found he couldn't wipe the haunted expression in her eyes from his mind, his pace faltering as he allowed himself to reflect fully on what had just happened.

Perhaps he'd been a bit too hard on her.

Running a hand over his tired eyes, he shook his head at himself. Who was he kidding—he'd definitely overreacted. For all he knew, it could have been a sick relative on the phone whom she needed to visit urgently.

The trouble was, he'd been so careful to

keep her at arm's length and not to let any of his own personal details slip he'd totally failed to ask her anything about herself.

And he was tired. So tired it was making him cranky.

Swivelling on the spot, he went back out of the room to find her, not entirely sure what he was going to say, but knowing he should probably smooth things over between them. He needed her on his side today.

Walking back towards the kitchen, he met her as she was coming out, a cup of tea in her hand.

Instead of the look of sheepish upset he'd expected to see, she gave him a bright smile.

'I know you have a conference call in a couple of minutes, so if you can walk me through what I need to tackle today I'll get straight on it,' she said, her voice steady and true as if the past few minutes hadn't happened.

He stared at her in surprise, unnerved by the one hundred and eighty degree turn in her demeanour.

Had he imagined the look in her eyes that had disturbed him so much?

No, it had definitely been there; he was sure of it.

Still, at least this showed she wasn't one to hold grudges and let an atmosphere linger after being reprimanded. He appreciated that. He certainly couldn't work with someone who struggled to maintain a professional front when something didn't go their way.

But her level of nonchalance confused him, leaving him a little unsure of where they now stood with each other. Should he mention that he felt he'd been a bit hard on her? Or should he just leave it and sweep it under the carpet as she seemed keen to do?

What was the matter with him? This was ridiculous. He didn't have time for semantics today.

Giving her a firm nod, he turned around and walked back towards the office. 'Good, let's get started then.'

Determined to keep her hand from shaking and not slop hot tea all over herself, Cara followed Max back into the office, ready to be given instructions for the day.

She knew she couldn't afford to show any weakness right now.

Based on her experiences with Max so far, she was pretty damn sure if he thought she wasn't up to the job he'd fire her on the spot and then she'd be left with absolutely nothing.

That was not going to happen to her today.

She needed this job, with its excellent wage and the prospect of a good reference from a well-respected businessman, to be able to stay here in London. All she had to do was keep her head down and stick it out here with him until she found another permanent position somewhere else. She had CVs out at a couple more places and with any luck another opportunity might present itself soon. Until then she'd just have to make sure she didn't allow his blunt manner and sharp tongue to erode her delicate confidence any further.

The trouble was, she'd allowed herself to be lulled into a false sense of security on her first day here after Max's compliment about her being a good ambassador for herself, only for him to pull the rug out from under her regrouping confidence later with his moods and quick temper.

The very last thing she needed was to work with another bully.

Not that she could really blame him for being angry in this instance. It must have looked really bad, her taking a personal phone call at the beginning of the working day. The really frustrating thing was that she'd never done anything like that before in her life. She was a rule follower to the core and very strict with herself about not surfing the Net or making personal calls on her employer's time, even in a big office where those kinds of things could go unnoticed.

Putting her drink down carefully, she wheeled her chair nearer to Max's desk and prepared to take notes, keeping her chin up and a benign smile fixed firmly on her face.

His own professional manner seemingly restored, Max outlined what he wanted her to do throughout the day, which she jotted down in her notebook. Once he appeared to be satisfied that he'd covered everything he leaned back in his chair and studied her, the intensity of his gaze making the hairs stand up on her arms.

'Listen, Cara, I'm finishing early for the day today,' he said, surprising her with the warmth in his voice. 'I'm meeting a friend in town for an early dinner, so feel free to leave here at four o'clock.'

She blinked at him in shock before pulling herself together. 'That would be great. Thank you.'

There was an uncomfortable pause, where he continued to look at her, his brows drawn together and his lips set in a firm line. He opened his mouth, as if he was about to tell her what was on his mind, but was rudely interrupted by the alarm going off on his phone signalling it was time for his conference call.

To her frustration, he snapped straight back into work mode, turning back to his computer and dialling a number on his phone, launching straight into his business spiel as soon as the person on the other end of the line picked up.

Despite her residual nerves, Cara still experienced the familiar little frisson of exhilaration that swept through her whenever she heard him do that. He'd set up a small desk for her next to his the day after he'd offered her the trial, which meant there was no getting away from the sound of his voice with its smooth, reassuring intonation.

He really was a very impressive businessman, even if he was a bit of a bear to work for.

Forcing her mind away from thinking about how uplifting it would be to have someone as passionate and dedicated as Max for a boyfriend—especially after the demeaning experience of her last relationship—she fired up her laptop and started in on the work he'd given her to take care of today.

After a few minutes, her thoughts drifted back to the fateful phone call she'd taken earlier, before their confrontation, and she felt a twitch of nerves in her stomach. It had been a friend calling to let her know about a possible flat coming onto the rental market— which was why she'd broken her rule and answered the call. If she managed to get there early enough she might just be able to snag it, which was now a real possibility thanks to Max's sudden announcement about leaving work at four o'clock.

Come to think of it, she was a little surprised about him finishing early to meet a friend in town. He'd never done that before, always continuing to work as she packed up for the day and—she strongly suspected—on into the evening. That would certainly account for the dark circles under his eyes. And his irascible mood.

The man appeared to be a workaholic.

After an hour of working through some

truly tedious data inputting, Cara got up to make them both a hot drink, aware that Max must be parched by now from having to talk almost continuously since he'd begun his call.

Returning with the drinks, she sat back down at her desk to see she had an email from the friend that had called her earlier about the flat for rent.

Hmm. That couldn't be a good sign; she'd already mailed the details through earlier.

With a sinking feeling, she opened it up and scanned the text, her previously restored mood slipping away.

The flat had already been let.

An irrational impulse to cry gripped her and she got up quickly and made for the bathroom before the tears came, desperate to hide her despondency from Max.

Staring into the mirror, she attempted to talk herself down from her gloom. Her friend Sarah had offered to put her up on her sofa for a few days, so she at least had somewhere to stay in the interim. The only trouble was, her friend lived in a tiny place that she shared with her party animal boyfriend and he wouldn't want her hanging around, playing gooseberry, for too long.

The mere idea of renting with strangers at the ripe old age of twenty-seven horrified her, so she was going to have to be prepared to lower her standards to be in with a chance of finding another one-bedroom flat that she could afford in central London.

That was okay; she could do that. Hopefully, something would come up soon and then she'd be able to make some positive changes and get fully back on her feet.

Surely it was time for things to start going her way now?

CHAPTER THREE

AFTER MAKING UP the excuse about seeing a friend on Friday night in order to let Cara leave early, Max decided that he might as well phone around to see if anyone was available for a pint after work and actually surprised himself by having an enjoyable night out with some friends that he hadn't seen for a while.

He'd spent the rest of the weekend working, only breaking to eat his way through the entire contents of the fridge that Cara had stocked for him. Despite his initial disdain at her choices, he found he actually rather enjoyed trying the things she'd bought. They certainly beat the mediocre takeaways he'd been living on for the past few months.

Perhaps it *was* useful for him to have someone else around the house for a while, as Poppy had suggested the last time they'd seen each other. He'd baulked at her proposal that he should get back out on the dating scene though—he definitely wasn't ready for that, and honestly couldn't imagine ever being ready.

He and Jemima had been a couple since meeting at the beginning of their first year at university, their initial connection so immediate and intense they'd missed lectures for three days running to stay in bed together. They'd moved in with each other directly after graduating, making a home for themselves first in Manchester, then in London. After spending so much of his youth being moved from city to city, school to school, by his bohemian mother—until he finally put his foot down and forced her to send him to boarding school—it had been a huge relief to finally feel in control of his own life. To belong somewhere, with someone who wouldn't ask him to give up the life and friends he'd painstakingly carved out for himself—just *one* more time.

Jemima had understood his need for stability and had put up with his aversion to change with sympathetic acceptance and generous bonhomie. His life had been comfortably settled and he'd been deeply content—until she'd died, leaving him marooned and devastated by grief.

The idea of finding someone he could love as much as Jem seemed ludicrous. No one could ever replace his wife and it wouldn't be fair to let them try.

No, he would be fine on his own; he had his business and his friends and that would be enough for him.

Walking past the flower arrangement that Cara had left on the hall table on his way to sort through yesterday's junk mail, he had a memory flash of the expression on her face when he'd bawled her out in the kitchen the other day.

His chest tightened uncomfortably at the memory.

He needed to stop beating himself up about that now. He'd made amends for what had happened, even if she hadn't seemed entirely back to her happy, bright-eyed self again by the time she'd left on Friday afternoon. But at least he hadn't needed to delve into the murky waters of how they were both *feeling* about what had happened. He'd had enough of that kind of thing after forcing himself through the interminable sessions with grief counsellors after Jemima's death; he certainly didn't need to put himself through that discomfort again for something as inconsequential as a spat with his employee.

Fortunately, Cara seemed as reluctant to talk about it all as he was.

Rubbing a hand over his face, he gave a snort of disbelief about where his thoughts had taken him. Again. Surely it wasn't normal to be spending his weekend thinking about his PA.

Hmm.

His initial concerns about her being an unwanted distraction seemed to be coming to fruition, which was a worry. Still, there were only a few more weeks left of the promised trial period, then he'd be free of her. Until then he was going to have to keep his head in the game, otherwise the business was going to suffer. And that wasn't something he was prepared to let happen.

Monday morning rushed around, bringing with it bright sunshine that flooded the house and warmed the still, cool air, lifting his spirits a little.

Max had just sat down at his desk with his

first cup of coffee of the day when there was a ring on the doorbell.

Cara.

Swinging open the door to let her in, he was taken aback to see her looking as if she hadn't slept a wink all night. There were dark circles around her puffy eyes and her skin was pallid and dull-looking. It seemed to pain her to even raise a smile for him.

Was she hung-over?

His earlier positivity vanished, to be replaced by a feeling of disquiet.

'Did you have a good weekend?' he asked as she walked into the house and hung up her coat.

She gave him a wan smile. 'Not bad, thanks. It was certainly a busy one. I didn't get much sleep.'

Hmm. So she had been out partying, by the sound of it.

Despite his concerns, Cara appeared to work hard all day and he only caught her yawning once whilst making them both a strong cup of coffee in the kitchen, mid-afternoon.

At the end of the day, she waved her usual cheery goodbye, though there was less enthusiasm in her smile than she normally displayed at knocking-off time.

To his horror, she turned up in the same state the following day.

And the next.

In fact, on Thursday, when he opened the door, he could have sworn he caught the smell of alcohol on her as she dashed past him into the house. She certainly looked as though she could have been up drinking all night and plainly hadn't taken a shower that morning, her hair hanging greasy and limp in a severely pulled back ponytail.

Her work was beginning to suffer too, in increments. Each day he found he had to pick her up on more and more things she'd missed or got wrong, noticing that her once pristine fingernails were getting shorter and more ragged as time went on.

Clearly she was letting whatever was happening in her personal life get in the way of her work and that was unacceptable.

His previous feelings of magnanimity about having her around had all but vanished by Thursday afternoon and he was seriously considering having a word with her about her performance. The only reason he hadn't done so already was because he'd been so busy with back-to-back conference calls this week and in deference to Poppy he'd decided to give Cara the benefit of the doubt and put her slip-ups down to a couple of off days.

But he decided that enough was enough when he found her with her head propped on her arms, fast asleep, on the kitchen table when she was supposed to be making them both a hot drink.

Resentment bubbled up from his gut as he watched her peaceful form gently rise and fall as she slumbered on, totally oblivious to his incensed presence behind her. He'd been feeling guilty all weekend about how he'd spoken to her on Friday and here she was, only a few days later, turning up unfit for work.

His concern that her presence here would cause more harm than good had just been ratified.

'Wakey, wakey, Sleeping Beauty!' he said loudly, feeling a swell of angry satisfaction as she leapt up from the table and spun around to look at him, her face pink and creased on one side where it had rested against her arm.

'Oh! Whoa! Was I sleeping?' she mumbled, blinking hard.

Crossing his arms, he gave her a hard stare. 'Like a baby.'

She rubbed a hand across her eyes, smudging her make-up across her face. 'I'm so sorry—I only put my head down to rest for a moment while I was waiting for the kettle to boil and I must have drifted off.'

'Perhaps you should start going to bed at a more reasonable time then,' he ground out, his hands starting to shake as adrenaline kicked its way through his veins. 'I didn't hire you as a charity case, Cara. For the money I'm paying, I expected much more from you. You had me convinced you were up to the job in the first couple of days, but it's become clear over the last few that you're not.' He took a breath as he made peace with what he was about to say. 'I'm going to have to let you go. I can't carry someone who's going to get drunk every night and turn up unfit to work.'

Her eyes were wide now and she was mouthing at him as if her response had got stuck in her throat.

Shaking off the stab of conscience that had begun to poke him in the back, he pointed a finger at her. 'And you can hold the "It'll never happen again" routine,' he bit out. 'I'm not an idiot, though I feel like one for letting you take me in like this.'

To his surprise, instead of the tears he was readying himself for, her expression morphed into one of acute fury and she raised her own shaking finger back at him.

'I do not get drunk every night. For your information, I'm homeless at the moment and sleeping on a friend's couch, which doesn't work well for her insomniac boyfriend, who likes to party and play computer games late into the night and who came home drunk and spilled an entire can of beer over me while I was trying to sleep and who then hogged the bathroom this morning so I couldn't get in there for a shower.'

Her face had grown redder and redder throughout this speech and all he could do was stand there and stare at her, paralysed by surprise as she jabbed her finger at him with rage flashing in her eyes.

'I've worked my butt off for you, taking your irascible moods on the chin and getting on with it, but I'm not going to let you treat me like some nonentity waster. I'm a real person with real feelings, Max. I tried to make this work—you have no idea how hard I've been trying—but I guess this is just life's way of telling me that I'm done here in London.' She threw up her hands and took a deep shaky breath. 'After all the work I put into building myself a career here that I was so proud of—'

Taking in the look of utter frustration on her face, he felt his anger begin to drain away, only to be replaced with an uncomfortable twist of shame.

She was right, of course—he had been really unfriendly and probably very difficult to work with, and she was clearly dealing with some testing personal circumstances, which he'd made sure to blithely ignore.

He frowned and sighed heavily, torn about what to do next. While he could do without any extra problems at the moment, he couldn't bring himself to turn her away now he knew what she was dealing with. Because, despite it all, he admired her for standing up for herself.

Cara willed her heart to stop pounding like a pneumatic drill as she waited to see what Max would say next.

Had she really just shouted at him like that?

It was so unlike her to let her anger get the better of her, but something inside her had snapped at the unfairness of it all and she hadn't been able to hold back.

After spending the past few days using every ounce of energy keeping up the fake smile and pretending she could cope with the punishing days with Max on so little sleep, she'd hit a wall.

Hard.

The mix of panic, frustration and chronic tiredness had released something inside her and in those moments after she'd let the words fly she had the strangest sensation of the ground shifting under her feet. She was painfully aware that she'd probably just thrown away any hope of keeping this job, but at the same time she was immensely proud of herself for not allowing him to dismiss her like that. As if she was worth nothing.

Because she *wasn't*.

She deserved to be treated with more respect and she'd learnt by now that she wasn't going to get that from Max by meekly taking the insults he so callously dished out.

At her last place of work, in a fug of naïve disbelief, she'd allowed those witches to strip her of her pride, but there was no way she was letting Max do that to her, too.

No matter what it cost her.

She could get another job—and she would, eventually—but she'd never be able to respect herself again if she didn't stand up to him now.

Her heart raced as she watched a range of expressions run across Max's face. The fact that he hadn't immediately repeated his dismissal gave her hope that there might be a slim chance he'd reverse his decision to fire her.

Moving her hands behind her back, she crossed her fingers for a miracle, feeling a bead of sweat run down her spine.

Sighing hard, Max ran a hand through the front of his hair, pushing it out of his eyes and looking at her with his usual expression of ill-concealed irritation.

'I'm guessing you became homeless on Friday, which is when the mistakes started to happen?' he asked finally.

She nodded, aware of the tension in her shoulders as she held her nerve. 'I spent all day on Sunday moving my furniture into storage.

I've been staying with my friend Sarah and her boyfriend ever since.'

'But that can't carry on,' he said with finality to his voice.

Swallowing hard, she tipped up her chin. 'No. I know. I've tried to view so many places to rent in the last week, but they seem to go the second they're advertised. I can't get to them fast enough.'

He crossed his arms. 'And you have nowhere else to stay in London? No boyfriend? No family?'

Shaking her head, she straightened her posture, determined to hang on to her poise. She wouldn't look away, not now she'd been brave enough to take him on. If she was going to be fired, she was going down with her head held high. 'My parents live in Cornwall and none of my other friends in London have room to put me up.' She shifted uncomfortably on the spot and swallowed back the lingering hurt at the memory of her last disastrous relationship. 'I've been single for a few months now.'

He stared back at her, his eyes hooded and his brow drawn down.

A world of emotions rattled through her as she waited to hear his verdict.

'Okay. You can stay here until you find a flat to rent.'

She gawped at him, wondering whether her brain was playing tricks on her. 'I'm sorry— *what*?'

'I said—you can stay here,' he said slowly, enunciating every word. 'I have plenty of spare rooms. I'm on the top floor so you could have the whole middle floor to yourself.'

'Really?'

He bristled, rolling his eyes up to the ceiling and letting out a frustrated snort. 'Yes, really. I'm not just making this up to see your impression of a goldfish.'

She stared at him even harder. Had he just made a *joke*? That was definitely a first.

Unfolding his arms, he batted a hand through the air. 'I'm sure it won't take you long to find somewhere else and until then I need you turning up to work fully rested and back to your efficient, capable self.'

Her eyes were so wide now she felt sure she must look as if she was wearing a pair of those joke goggle-eye glasses.

He was admitting to her being good at her job too now? Wonders would never cease.

But she was allowing these revelations to

distract her from the decision she needed to make. Could she really live in the same house as her boss? Even if it was only for a short time.

Right now, it didn't feel as though she had much of a choice. The thought of spending even one more night in Party Central made her heart sink. If she turned Max down on his offer, that was the only other viable option—save staying in a hotel she couldn't afford or renting a place a long way out and spending her life commuting in. Neither of them were appealing options.

But could she really live here with him? The mere idea of it made her insides flutter and it wasn't just because he was a bit of a difficult character. During the week and a half that she'd known him, she'd become increasingly jittery in his presence, feeling a tickle of excitement run up her spine every time she caught his scent in the air or even just watched him move around his territory like some kind of lean, mean, business machine. Not that he'd ever given her a reason to think she was in any kind of danger being there alone with him. Clearly, he had no interest in her romantically. If anything, she'd felt it had been the total opposite for him, as if he didn't think of her as a woman at all, only a phone-answering, data-sorting robot.

So she was pretty sure he didn't have an ulterior motive behind his suggestion that she should stay in his house.

Unfortunately.

Naughty, naughty Cara.

'Well, if you're sure it won't be too much of an inconvenience to you,' she said slowly.

'No. It's fine,' he answered curtly. 'We'll have to make sure to respect each other's privacy, but it's a big place so that shouldn't be a problem. All the rooms have locks on them, in case you're worried.'

Her pulse picked up as a host of X-rated images rushed through her head.

Slam a lid on that, you maniac.

'I'm not worried,' she squeaked.

He nodded.

'And your girlfriend won't mind me staying here?' she asked carefully.

'I don't have a girlfriend.'

'Or your w—?' she began to ask, just in case.

'I'm single,' he cut in with a curt snap to his voice.

Okay, so the subject of his relationships was out of bounds then.

She was surprised to hear that he wasn't attached in any way, though. Surely someone with his money, looks and smarts would have women lining up around the block for the pleasure of his company. Although, come to think of it, based on her run-ins with him so far, she could see how his acerbic temperament might be a problem for some people.

'Right, I may as well show you your room now,' Max said, snapping her out of her meandering thoughts. 'Clearly, you're not in a fit state to work this afternoon, so you may as well finish for the day.' He turned and walked out of the room, leaving her gaping at the empty space he'd left.

So that was it then—decision made.

'Oh! Okay.' She hustled to catch him up, feeling her joints complain as she moved. *Crikey.* She was tired. Her whole body ached from sleeping on a saggy sofa and performing on so little sleep for the past few days.

She followed him up the sweeping staircase to the next level and along the landing to the third door on the right.

Opening it up, he motioned for her to walk past him into the bedroom.

She tried not to breathe in his fresh, spicy scent as she did so, her nerves already shot from the rigours of the day.

It was, of course, the most beautifully appointed bedroom she'd ever been in.

Light flooded in through the large window, which was framed by long French grey curtains in a heavy silk. The rest of the furnishing was simple and elegant, in a way Cara had never been able to achieve in her own flat. The pieces that had been chosen clearly had heritage and fitted perfectly with the large airy room. His interior designer must have cost a pretty penny.

Tears welled in her eyes as she took in the original ornate fireplace, which stood proudly opposite a beautiful king-sized iron-framed bed. Fighting the urge to collapse onto it in relief and bury herself in the soft, plump-looking duvet, she blinked hard, then turned to face Max, who was hanging back by the door with a distracted frown on his face.

'This is a beautiful room—thank you,' she said, acutely aware of the tremor in her voice.

Max's frown deepened, but he didn't comment on it. 'You're welcome. You should go over to your friend's house and get your things now, then you'll have time to settle in. We'll start over again tomorrow.'

'Okay, good idea.'

'I'll leave you to it then,' he said, turning to go.

'Max?'

He turned back. 'Yes?'

'I'm really grateful—for letting me stay here.'

'No problem,' he said, turning briskly on the spot and walking away, leaving her staring after him with her heart in her mouth.

Well, she certainly hadn't expected this when she'd woken up this morning reeking of stale beer.

Sinking down gratefully onto the bed, she finally allowed her tense muscles to relax, feeling the tiredness rush back, deep into her bones.

How was she ever going to be able to drag herself away from this beautiful room when she managed to find a place of her own to rent?

More to the point, was she really going to be able to live in the same house as Max without going totally insane?

Steeling herself to make the journey over to Sarah's house and pick up her things, she rocked herself up off the bed of her dreams and onto her feet and took a deep, resolute breath.

There was only one way to find out.

CHAPTER FOUR

IF SOMEONE HAD asked Max to explain exactly what had prompted him to suggest that Cara move in, he was pretty sure he'd have been stumped for an answer.

All he knew was that he couldn't let things go on the way they were. Judging by her outburst, she was clearly struggling to cope with all that life had thrown at her recently and it was no skin off his nose to let her stay for a few nights in one of the empty bedrooms.

He had enough of them, after all.

Also, as a good friend of her cousin's he felt a responsibility to make sure that Cara was okay whilst Poppy was away and unable to help her herself. He knew from experience that good friends were essential when life decided to throw its twisted cruelty your way, and he was acutely aware that it was the support and encouragement of his friends that had helped him find his way out of the darkness after Jemima died.

Watching Cara working hard the next day, he was glad she was still around. When she was on good form, she was an asset to the business and, truthfully, it had become comforting for him to have another person around—it stopped him from *thinking* so much in the resounding silence of the house.

They hadn't talked about what had happened again, which was a relief. He just wanted everything to get back to the way it had been with the minimum of fuss. With that in mind, he was a little concerned about what it would be like having her around at the weekend. He'd probably end up working, like he always did, so he wasn't too worried about the daytime, but they'd need to make sure they gave each other enough space in the evenings so they didn't end up biting each other's heads off again.

With any luck, she'd be out a lot of the time anyway, flat-hunting or seeing friends.

At six o'clock he leant back in his chair and stretched his arms above his head, working the kinks out of his tight muscles.

'Time to finish for the day, Cara,' he said to the side of her head.

She glanced round at him, the expression in her eyes far away, as if she was in the middle of a thought.

'Um, okay. I'll just finish this.' She tapped on her keyboard for a few more seconds before closing the laptop with a flourish.

'Okay then. Bring on the weekend.' She flashed him a cheeky smile, which gave him pause.

'You're not thinking of bringing the party to this house, I hope.'

Quickly switching to a solemn expression, she gave a shake of her head. 'Of course not. That's not what I meant.'

'Hmm.'

The corner of her mouth twitched upwards. 'You seem to have a really skewed impression of me. I don't go in for heavy drinking and partying—it's really not my style.'

'Okay.' He held up both hands. 'Not that it's any of my business; you can stay out all night at the weekends, for all I care,' he said, aware of a strange plummeting sensation in his chest as images of what she might get up to out on the town flashed through his head.

Good God, man—you're not her keeper.

'As long as your work doesn't suffer,' he added quickly.

'Actually,' she said, slouching back in her seat and hooking her slender arm over the back of her chair, 'I was thinking about cooking you a meal tonight, to say thank you for letting me stay.'

He wasn't sure why, but the thought of that made him uncomfortable. Perhaps because it would blur the lines between employee and friend too much.

'That's kind, but I have plans tonight,' he lied, racking his brain to remember what his friend Dan had said about his availability this weekend. Even if he was busy he was sure he could rustle up a dinner invitation somewhere else, to let Cara off the hook without any bad feelings.

'And you don't need to thank me for letting you stay here. It's what any decent human being would have done.'

Her face seemed to fall a little and she drew her arm back in towards her body, sliding her hands between her knees so that her shoulders hunched inwards. 'Oh, okay, well, I'm just going to pop out and shop for my own dinner, so I'll see you shortly,' she said, ramping her smile back up again and wheeling her chair away from the desk with her feet.

'Actually, I'm heading out myself in a minute and I'll probably be back late, so I'll see you tomorrow.'

Her smile froze. 'Right. Well, have a good night.'

This was ridiculous. The last thing he'd wanted was for them both to feel awkward about living under the same roof.

He let out a long sigh and pushed his hair away from his face. 'Look, Cara, don't think you have to hang out with me while you're staying here. We don't need to be in each other's pockets the whole time. Feel free to do your own thing.'

Clearly he'd been a bit brusque because she recoiled a little. 'I understand,' she said, getting up and awkwardly pushing her chair back under her desk. 'Have a good night!' she said in that overly chirpy way she had, which he was beginning to learn meant he'd offended her.

Not waiting for his reply, she turned her back on him and walked straight out of the room, her shoulders stiff.

Great. This was exactly what he'd hoped to avoid.

He scrubbed a hand over his face. Maybe it had been a mistake to ask her to stay.

But he couldn't kick her out now.

All he could do was cross his fingers and hope she'd find herself another place to live soon.

To his surprise, he didn't see much of Cara over the next couple of days. She'd obviously taken his suggestion about giving each other space to heart and was avoiding being in the house with him as much as possible.

The extremity of her desertion grated on his nerves.

What was it that made it impossible for them to understand each other? They were very different in temperament, of course, which didn't help, but it was more than that. It was as if there was some kind of meaning-altering force field between them.

On Sunday, when the silence in the house got too much for him, he went out for a long walk around Hyde Park. He stopped at the café next to the water for lunch, something he and Jemima had done most Sundays, fight-

ing against the painful undertow of nostalgia
that dragged at him as he sat there alone. It
was all so intensely familiar.

All except for the empty seat in front of
him.

He snorted into his drink, disgusted with
himself for being so pathetic. He should
consider himself lucky. He was the one who
got to have a future, unlike his big-hearted,
selfless wife. The woman who everyone had
loved. One of the few people, in his opinion,
who had truly deserved a long and happy life.

Arriving home mid-afternoon, he walked
in to find the undertones of Cara's perfume
hanging in the air.

So she was back then.

Closing his eyes, he imagined he could actually sense her presence in the atmosphere,
like a low hum of white noise.

Or was he being overly sensitive?

Probably.

From the moment she'd agreed to move in
he'd experienced a strange undercurrent of
apprehension and it seemed to be affecting
his state of mind.

After stowing his shoes and coat in the
cloakroom, he went into the living room to

find that a large display of flowers had been placed on top of the grand piano. He bristled, remembering the way he'd felt the last time Cara had started to mess with his environment.

Sighing, he rubbed a hand through his hair, attempting to release the tension in his scalp. They were just flowers. He really needed to chill out or he was going to drive himself insane. Jemima would have laughed if she'd seen how strung-out he was over something so inconsequential. He could almost hear her teasing voice ringing in his ears.

A noise startled him and he whipped round to see Cara standing in the doorway to the room, dressed in worn jeans and a sloppy sweater, her face scrubbed of make-up and her bright blue eyes luminous in the soft afternoon light. To his overwrought brain, she seemed to radiate an ethereal kind of beauty, her long hair lying in soft, undulating waves around her face and her creamy skin radiant with health. He experienced a strangely intense moment of confusion, and he realised that somewhere in the depths of his screwed-up consciousness he'd half expected it to be Jemima standing there instead—which was why his, 'Hello,' came out more gruffly than he'd intended.

Her welcoming smile faltered and she glanced down at her fingernails and frowned, as if fighting an impulse to chew on them, but when she looked back up her smile was firmly back in place.

'Isn't it a beautiful day?' She tipped her head towards the piano behind him. 'I hope you don't mind, but the spring sunshine inspired me to put fresh flowers in most of the rooms—not your bedroom, of course; I didn't go in there,' she added quickly. 'The house seemed to be crying out for a bit of life and colour and I wanted to do something to say thank you for letting me stay, even though you said I didn't need to.'

'Sure. That's fine,' was all he could muster. For some reason his blood was flying through his veins and he felt so hot he thought he might spontaneously combust at any second.

'Oh, and I stripped and remade the bed in the room next to yours,' she added casually. 'It looked like the cleaners had missed it. I gave it a good vacuum, too; it was really dusty.'

The heat was swept away by a flood of icy panic. 'You *what*?'

The ferocity in his tone obviously alarmed her because she flinched and blinked hard.

But hurting Cara's feelings was the least of his worries right then.

Not waiting for her reply, he pushed past her and raced up the stairs, aware of his heart thumping painfully in his chest as he willed it not to be so.

Please don't let her have destroyed that room.

Reaching the landing on the top floor, he flung open the door and stared into the now immaculate bedroom, the stringent scent of cleaning fluid clogging his throat and making his stomach roll.

She'd stripped it bare.

Everything he'd been protecting from the past had been torn off or wiped away. The bed, as she'd said, now had fresh linen on it.

He heard her laboured breath behind him as she made it up to the landing and whipped round to face her.

'Where are the sheets from the bed, Cara?' he demanded, well past the point of being able to conceal his anger.

Her face was drained of all colour. 'What did I do wrong?'

'The *sheets*, Cara—where are the *sheets*?'

'I washed them,' she whispered, unable to meet his eyes. 'They're in the dryer.'

That was it then. Jemima's room was ruined.

Bitterness welled in his gut as he took in her wide-eyed bewilderment. The woman was a walking disaster area and she'd caused nothing but trouble since she got here.

A rage he couldn't contain made him pace towards her.

'Why do you have to meddle with everything? Hmm? What is it with you? This need to please all the time isn't natural. In fact it's downright pathetic. Just keep your hands off my personal stuff, okay? Is that really too much to ask?'

She seemed frozen to the spot as she stared at him with glassy eyes, her jaw clamped so tight he could see the muscle flickering under the pressure, but, instead of shouting back this time, she dragged in a sharp, painful-sounding breath before turning on the spot and walking out of the room.

He listened to her heavy footsteps on the

stairs and then the slam of her bedroom door, wincing as the sound reverberated through his aching head. Staring down at the soulless bed, he allowed the heat of his bitterness and anger and shame to wash through him, leaving behind an icy numbness in its wake.

Then he closed his eyes, dropped his chin to his chest and sank down onto the last place he'd been truly happy.

Oh, God, please don't let this be happening to me. Again.

Cara wrapped her arms around her middle and pressed her forehead against the cool wall of her bedroom, waiting for the dizziness and nausea to subside so she could pack up her things and leave.

What was it with her? She seemed destined to put herself in a position of weakness, where the only option left to her was to give up and run away.

Which she really didn't want to do again.

But she had to protect herself. She couldn't be around someone so toxic—someone who clearly thought so little of her. Even Ewan hadn't been that cruel to her when he'd left her after she'd failed to live up to his exact-

ing standards. She'd never seen a look of such
pure disgust on anyone's face before. The
mere memory of it made the dizziness worse.

There was no way she was staying in a
place where she'd be liable to see that look
again. She'd rather go home and admit to her
parents that she'd failed and deal with their
badly concealed disappointment than stay
here with Max any longer.

She'd never met anyone with such a quick
temper. What was his problem, anyway? He
appeared to have everything here: the security of a beautiful house in one of the most
sought-after areas of London, a thriving business, friends who invited him out for dinner,
and he clearly had pots of cash to cushion
his easy, comfortable life. In fact, the more
she thought about it, the more incensed she
became.

Who was he to speak to her like that? Sure,
there had been a couple of little bumps in the
road when she'd not exactly been at her best,
but she'd worked above and beyond the call
of duty for the rest of the time. And she'd
been trying to do something nice for him in
making the house look good—pretty much
the only thing she could think of to offer as a

thank you to a man who seemed to have everything. What had been so awful about that? She knew she could be a bit over the top in trying to please people sometimes, but this hadn't been a big thing. It was just an empty guest room that had been overlooked.

Wasn't it?

The extremity of his reaction niggled at her.

Surely just giving it a quick clean didn't deserve that angry reaction.

No.

He was a control freak bully and she needed to get away from him.

As soon as she was sure the dizziness had passed, she carefully packed up all her things and zipped them into her suitcase, fighting with all her might against the tight pressure in her throat and the itchy heat in her eyes.

She'd known this opportunity had to be too good to be true—the job, working with someone as impressive as Max and definitely being invited to stay in this amazing house.

But she wasn't going to skulk away. If she didn't face up to Max one last time with her head held high she'd regret it for the rest of her life. He wasn't going to run her out of here; she was going to leave in her time and on her terms.

Taking a deep breath, she rolled her shoulders back and fixed the bland look of calm she'd become so practised at onto her face.

Okay. Time for one last confrontation.

She found Max in the guest room where she'd left him, sitting on the bed with his head in his hands, his hunched shoulders stretching his T-shirt tight against his broad back.

As she walked into the room, he looked up at her with an expression of such torment on his face that it made her stop in her tracks.

What was going on? She'd expected him to still be angry, but instead he looked—*beaten*.

Did he regret what he'd said to her?

Giving herself a mental shake, she took another deliberate step towards him. It didn't matter; there wasn't anything he could say to make up for the cruelty of his last statement anyway. This wasn't the first time he'd treated her with such brutal disdain and she wasn't going to put up with it any longer.

Forcing back her shoulders, she took one final step closer to him, feeling her legs shaking with tension.

'This isn't going to work, Max. I can't live

in a place where I'm constantly afraid of doing the wrong thing and making you angry. I don't know what I did that was so bad, or what's going on with you to make you react like that, but I'm not going to let you destroy what's left of my confidence. I'm not going to be a victim any more.' She took a deep, shuddering breath. 'So I'm leaving now. And that goes for the job, too.'

Her heart gave a lurch at the flash of contrition in his eyes, but she knew she had to be strong and walk away for her own good.

'Goodbye, Max, and good luck.'

As she turned to go, fighting against the tears that threatened to give her away, she thought she heard the bedsprings creak as if he'd stood up, but didn't turn round to find out.

She was halfway down the stairs when she heard Max's voice behind her. 'Wait, Cara!'

Spinning round, she held up a hand to stop him from coming any closer, intensely aware that, despite her anger with him, there was a small part of her that was desperate to hear him say something nice to her, to persuade her that he wasn't the monster he seemed to be. 'I can't walk on eggshells around you any more, Max; I don't think my heart will stand it.'

In any way, shape or form.

He slumped down onto the top step and put his elbows on his knees, his whole posture defeated. 'Don't go,' he said quietly.

'I have to.'

Looking up, he fixed her with a glassy stare. 'I know I've been a nightmare to be around recently—' He frowned and shook his head. 'It's not you, Cara—it's one hundred per cent me. Please, at least hear me out. I need to tell you what's going on so you don't leave thinking any of this is your fault.' He sighed and rubbed a hand through his hair. 'That's the last thing I want to happen.'

She paused. Even if she still chose to leave after hearing him out, at least she'd know *why* it hadn't worked and be able to make peace with her decision to walk away.

The silence stretched to breaking point between them. 'Okay,' she said.

He nodded. 'Thank you.' Getting up from the step, he gestured down the stairs. 'Let's go into the sitting room.'

Once there, she perched on the edge of the sofa and waited for him to take the chair opposite, but he surprised her by sitting next to her instead, sinking back into the cushions with a long guttural sigh which managed to touch every nerve-ending in her body.

'This is going to make me sound mentally unstable.'

She turned to frown at him. 'Oka-ay…' she said, failing to keep her apprehension out of her voice.

'That bed hasn't been changed since my wife, Jemima, died a year and a half ago.'

Hot horror slid through her, her skin prickling as if she were being stabbed with a thousand needles. 'But I thought you said—' She shook her suddenly fuzzy head. 'You never said—' Words, it seemed, had totally failed her. Everything she knew about him slipped sickeningly into place: the ever-fluctuating moods, the reluctance to talk about his personal life, his anger at her meddling with things in his house.

His *wife's* house.

Looking away, he stared at the wall opposite, sitting forward with clenched fists as if he was steeling himself to get it all out in the open.

'I couldn't bring myself to change it.' He

paused and she saw his shoulders rise then fall as he took a deep breath. 'The bed, I mean. It still smelled faintly like her. I let her mother take all her clothes and other personal effects—what would I have done with them?—but the bed was mine. The last place we'd been together before I lost her—' he took another breath, pushing back his hunched shoulders '—before she died.'

'Oh, God, Max… I'm so, so sorry. I had no idea.'

He huffed out a dry laugh. 'How could you? I did everything I could to avoid talking to you about it.' He grimaced. 'Because, to be honest, I've done enough talking about it to last me a lifetime. I guess, in my twisted imagination, I thought if you didn't know, I could pretend it hadn't happened when you were around. Outside of work, you're the first normal, unconnected thing I've had in my life since I lost her and I guess I was hanging on to that.'

He turned to look at her again. 'I should have told you, Cara, especially after you moved in, but I couldn't find a way to bring it up without—' He paused and swallowed hard, the look in his eyes so wretched that, without thinking, she reached out and laid a hand on his bare forearm.

He frowned down at where their bodies connected and the air seemed to crackle around them.

Disconcerted by the heat of him beneath her fingertips, she withdrew her hand and laid it back on her lap.

'It's kind of you to consider me *normal*,' she said, flipping him a grin, hoping the levity might go some way to smoothing out the sudden weird tension between them.

He gave a gentle snort, as if to acknowledge her pathetic attempt at humour.

Why had she never recognised his behaviour as grief before? Now she knew to look for it, it was starkly discernible in the deep frown lines in his face and the haunted look in his eyes.

But she'd been so caught up in her own private universe of problems she hadn't even considered *why* Max seemed so bitter all the time.

She'd thought he had everything.

How wrong she'd been.

They sat in silence for a while, the only sound in the room the soothing *tick-tock* of the carriage clock on the mantelpiece, like a steady heartbeat in the chaos.

'How did she die?' Cara asked eventually. She was pretty sure he wouldn't be keen to revisit this conversation and she wanted to have all the information from this point onwards so she could avoid any future blunders.

The familiarity of the question seemed to rouse him. 'She had a subarachnoid haemorrhage—it's where a blood vessel in the brain bursts—' he added, when she frowned at him in confusion. 'On our one-year wedding anniversary. It happened totally out of the blue. I was late for our celebration dinner and I got a phone message saying she'd collapsed in the restaurant. By the time I got to the hospital she had such extensive brain damage she didn't even recognise me. She died two weeks later. I never got to say goodbye properly.' He snorted gently. 'The last thing I said to her before it happened was "Stop being such a nag; I won't be late," when I left her in bed that morning and went to work.'

Cara had to swallow past the tightness in her throat before she could speak. 'That's why you didn't want me to leave here with us on bad terms.' She put a hand back onto his arm and gave it an ineffectual rub, feeling completely out of her depth. 'Oh, Max, I'm so sorry. What a horrible thing to happen.'

He leant back against the cushions, breaking the contact of her touch, and stared up at the ceiling. 'I often wonder whether I would have noticed some signs if I'd paid more attention to her. If I hadn't been so caught up with work—'

She couldn't think of a single thing to say to make him feel better—though maybe there wasn't anything she could say. Sometimes you didn't need answers or solutions; you just needed someone to listen and agree with you about how cruel life could be.

He turned to look at her, his mouth drawn into a tight line.

'Look, Cara, I can see that you wanting to help comes from a good place. You're a kind and decent person—much more decent than I am.' He gave her a pained smile, which she returned. 'I've been on my own here for so long I've clearly become very selfish with my personal space.' He rubbed a hand across his brow. 'And this was Jemima's house—she was the one who chose how to decorate it and made it a home for us.' He turned to make full eye contact with her again, his expression apologetic. 'It's taking a bit of adjusting to, having someone else around. Despite evidence to the contrary, I really appreciate the thoughtful gestures you've made.'

His reference to her *gestures* only made the heavy feeling in her stomach worse.

'I'm really sorry, Max. I can totally understand why you'd find it hard to see me meddling with Jemima's things. I think I was so excited by the idea of living in such a beautiful house that I got a bit carried away. I forgot I was just a visitor here and that it's your home. That was selfish of *me*.'

He shook his head. 'I don't want you to feel like that. While you're here it's your home, too.'

She frowned and turned away to stare down at the floor, distracted for a moment by how scratty and out of place her old slippers looked against the rich cream-coloured wool carpet.

That was exactly the problem. It wasn't her home and it never would be. She didn't really *fit* here.

For some reason that made her feel more depressed than she had since the day she'd left her last job.

'Have you had any luck with finding a flat to rent?' he asked, breaking the silence that had fallen like a suffocating layer of dust between them.

'Not yet, but I have an appointment to view somewhere tomorrow and there are new places coming up all the time. I'll find something soon, I'm sure of it,' she said, plastering what must have been the worst fake smile she'd ever mustered onto her face.

He nodded slowly, but didn't say anything.

Twitching with discomfort now, she stood up. 'I should go.'

He frowned at her in confusion. 'What do you mean? Where are you going?'

'Back to Sarah's. I think that would be best.'

Standing up, too, he put out a hand as if to touch her, but stopped himself and shoved it into the back pocket of his jeans instead.

'Look, don't leave. I promise to be less of an ogre. I let my anger get the better of me, which was unfair.'

'I don't know, Max—' She couldn't stay here now. Could she?

Obviously seeing the hesitation on her face, he leant forward and waited until she made eye contact. 'I like having you around.' There was a teasing lightness in his expression that made her feel as if he was finally showing her the real Max. The one who had been hiding inside layers of brusque aloofness and icy calm for the past few weeks.

Warmth pooled, deep in her body. 'Really? I feel like I've made nothing but a nuisance of myself since I got here.'

He gave another snort and the first proper smile she'd seen in a while. It made his whole face light up and the sight of it sent a rush of warm pleasure across her skin. 'It's certainly been *eventful* having you here.'

She couldn't help but return his grin, despite the feeling that she was somehow losing control of herself.

'Stay. Please.'

Her heart turned over at the expression on his face. It was something she'd never seen before. Against all the odds, he looked *hopeful*.

Despite a warning voice in the back of her head, she knew there was no way she could walk out of the door now that he'd laid himself bare. She could see that the extreme mood swings were coming from a place of deep pain and the very last thing he needed

was to be left alone with just his torment-
ing memories for company in this big empty
house.

It appeared as though they needed each
other.

The levelling of the emotional stakes gal-
vanised her.

'Okay,' she said, giving him a reassuring
smile. 'I'll stay. On one condition.'

'And that is?'

'That you *talk* to me when you feel the
gloom descending—like a *person*, not just
an employee. And let me help if I can.' She
crossed her arms and raised a challenging
eyebrow.

He huffed out a laugh. 'And how do you
propose to help?'

'I don't know. Perhaps I can jolly you out
of your moods, if you give me the chance.'

'*Jolly*. That's a fitting word for you.'

'Yeah, well, someone has to raise the positivity levels in this house of doom.' She
stilled, wondering whether she'd gone a step
too far, but when she dared to peek at him he
was smiling, albeit in a rather bemused way.

A sense of relief washed over her. The last
thing she wanted to do was read the situa-

tion wrong now they'd had a breakthrough. In fact, she really ought to push for a treaty to make things crystal clear between them.

'Look, at the risk of micromanaging the situation, can we agree that from this point on you'll be totally straight with me, and in return I promise to be totally straight with you?'

He gave her a puzzled look. 'Why? Is there something you need to tell me?'

She considered admitting she'd lied about why she'd left her last job and dismissed it immediately. There was no point going over that right now; it had no relevance to this and it would make her sound totally pathetic compared to what he'd been through.

'No, no! Nothing! It was just a turn of phrase.'

He snorted gently, rolling his eyes upward, his mouth lifting at the corner. 'Okay then, Miss Fix-it, total honesty it is. You've got yourself a deal.'

CHAPTER FIVE

JUST AS MAX thought he'd had enough drama to last him a lifetime, things took another alarming turn, only this time it was the business that threatened to walk away from him.

Opening his email first thing on Monday morning, he found a missive from his longest standing and most profitable client, letting him know that they were considering taking their business elsewhere.

Cara walked in with their coffee just as he'd finished reading it and the concern on her face made it clear how rattled he must look.

'Max? What's wrong?'

'Our biggest client is threatening to terminate our contract with them.'

Her eyes grew larger. 'Why?'

'I'm guessing one of our competitors has been sniffing around, making eyes at them and I've been putting off going to the meetings they've been trying to arrange for a while now. I haven't had the time to give them the same level of attention as before, so their head's been turned.'

'Is it salvageable?'

'Yes. If I go up there today and show them exactly why they should stay with me.'

'Okay.' She moved swiftly over to her desk and opened up her internet browser, her nails rattling against her keyboard as she typed in an enquiry. 'There's a train to Manchester in forty minutes. You go and pack some stuff; I'll call a cab and book you a seat. You can speak to me from the train about anything that needs handling today.'

He sighed and rubbed a hand through his hair, feeling the tension mounting in his scalp. 'It's going to take more than an afternoon to get this sorted. I'll probably need to be up there for most of the week.'

'Then stay as long as you need.'

Shaking his head, he batted a hand towards his computer. 'I have that proposal to finish for the end of Thursday, not to mention the monstrous list of things to tackle for all the other clients this week.'

'Leave it with me. If you set me up with a folder of your previous proposals and give me the questions you need answering, I'll put some sections together for you, so you'll only need to check and edit them as we go. And don't worry about the other clients; I can handle the majority of enquiries and rearrange anything that isn't urgent for next week. I'll only contact you with the really important stuff.'

'Are you sure you can handle that? It's a lot to leave you with at such short notice.'

'I'll be fine.' She seemed so eager he didn't have the heart to argue.

In all honesty, it was going to be tough for him to let go of his tight grip on the business and trust that this would work out, but he knew he didn't have a choice—there was no way he was letting this contract slip through his fingers. He really couldn't afford to lose this firm's loyalty at this point in his business's infancy; it would make him look weak to competitors as well as potential new clients, and presenting a confident front was everything in this game.

'Okay.' He stood up and gathered his laptop and charger together before making for

the door. 'Thanks, Cara. I'll get my stuff together and call you from the train.'

Turning back, he saw she was standing
stiffly with her hands clasped in front of her,
her eyes wide and her cheeks flushed.

Pausing for a moment, he wondered
whether he was asking too much of her, but
quickly dismissed it. She'd chosen to stay and
she knew what she was getting herself into.

They were in it together now.

To his relief, Cara successfully held the fort
back in London whilst he was away, routinely
emailing him sections of completed work to
be used in the business proposal that he wrote
in the evenings in time to make the deadline.
She seemed to have a real flair for picking out
relevant information and had made an excellent job of copying his language style.

She also saved his hide by sending flowers
and a card in his name to his mother for her
birthday, which he was ashamed to discover
he'd forgotten all about in his panic about losing the client.

Damaging the precarious cordiality that he
and his mother had tentatively built up after
working through their differences over the

past few years would have been just as bad, and he was immensely grateful to Cara for her forethought and care.

She really was excellent at her job.

In fact, after receiving compliments from clients about how responsive and professional she'd been when they'd contacted her with enquiries and complications to be dealt with, he was beginning to realise that he'd actually been very fortunate to secure her services. He felt sure, if she wanted to, she could walk into a job with a much better salary with her eyes shut.

Which made him wonder again why she hadn't.

Whatever the reason, the idea of losing her excellent skill base now made him uneasy. Even though he'd been certain he'd want to let her go at the end of the trial month, he was now beginning to think that that would be a huge mistake.

He had some serious thinking to do.

If he was honest, he reflected on Thursday evening, sitting alone in the hotel's busy restaurant, having time and space away from Cara and the house had been a relief. He'd been glad of the opportunity to get his head together after their confrontation. She was the first person, outside his close circle of friends, that he'd talked to in any detail about what had happened to Jemima and it had changed the atmosphere between them. To Cara's credit, she hadn't trotted out platitudes to try and make him feel better and he was grateful to her for that, but he felt a little awkward about how much of himself he'd exposed.

Conversely, though, it also felt as though a weight that he'd not noticed carrying had been lifted from his shoulders. Not just because he'd finally told Cara about Jem—which he'd begun to feel weirdly seedy about, as if he was keeping a dirty secret from her—but also because it had got to the point where he'd become irrationally superstitious about clearing out the room, as though all his memories of Jemima would be wiped away if he touched it. Which, of course, they hadn't been—she was still firmly embedded there in his head and his heart. So, even though he'd been angry and upset with Cara at the time, in retrospect, it had been a healthy thing for that decision to be wrenched out of his hands.

It felt as though he'd taken a step further into the light.

Cara was out when he arrived back at Friday lunchtime, still buzzed with elation from keeping the client, so he went to unpack his bags upstairs, return a few phone calls and take a shower before coming back down.

Walking into the kitchen, he spotted her standing by the sink with her back to him, washing a mug. He stopped to watch her for a moment, smiling as he realised she was singing softly to herself, her slim hips swaying in time to the rhythm of the song. She had a beautiful voice, lyrical and sweet, and a strange, intense warmth wound through him as he stood there listening to her. It had been a long time since anyone had sung in this house and there was something so pure and uplifting about it a shiver ran down his spine, inexplicably chased by a deep pull of longing.

Though not for Cara, surely? But for a time when his life had fewer sharp edges. A simpler time. A happier one.

Shaking himself out of this unsettling observation, he moved quickly into the room so she wouldn't think he'd been standing there spying on her.

'Hi, Cara.'

She jumped and gasped, spinning round to

face him, her hand pressed to her chest. She looked fresh and well rested, but there was a wary expression in her eyes.

'Max! I didn't hear you come in.'

'I was upstairs, taking a shower and returning some urgent calls. I got back about an hour ago.'

She nodded, her professional face quickly restored. 'How was Manchester?'

'Good. We got them back on board. How have things been here?'

'That's great! Things have been fine here. It's certainly been very quiet without you.'

By 'quiet' he suspected she actually meant less fraught with angry outbursts.

There was an uncomfortable silence while she fussed about with the tea towel, hooking it carefully over the handle of the cooker door and smoothing it until it lay perfectly straight.

Tearing his eyes away from the rather disconcerting sight of her stroking her hands slowly up and down the offending article, he walked over to where the kettle sat on the work surface and flicked it on to boil. He was unsettled to find that things still felt awkward between them when they were face to face—not that he should be surprised that they were.

Their last non-work conversation had been a pretty heavy one, after all.

Evidently he needed to make more of an effort to be friendly now if he was going to be in with a chance of persuading her to stay after the month's trial was up.

The thought of going back to being alone in this house certainly wasn't a comforting one any more. If he was honest, it had been heartening to know that Cara would be here when he got back. Now that the black hole of Jemima's room had been destroyed and he'd fully opened the door to Cara, the loneliness he'd previously managed to keep at bay had walked right in.

Turning to face her again, he leant back against the counter and crossed his arms.

'I wanted to talk to you about the quality of the work you've been producing.'

Her face seemed to pale and he realised he could have phrased that better. He'd never been good at letting his colleagues know when he was pleased with their work—or Jemima when he was proud of something she'd achieved, he realised with a stab of pain—but after Cara had given it to him straight about how it affected her, he was determined to get better at it.

'What I mean is—I'm really impressed with the way you've handled the work here this week while I've been away,' he amended.

'Oh! Good. Thank you.' The pride in her wobbly smile made his breath catch.

He nodded and gave a little cough to release the peculiar tension in his throat, turning back to the counter to grab a mug for his drink and give them both a moment to regroup. There was a brightly coloured card propped up next to the mug tree and he picked it up as a distraction while he waited for the kettle to finish boiling and glanced at what was written inside.

'You didn't tell me it was your birthday,' he said, turning to face her again, feeling an unsettling mixture of surprise and dismay at her not mentioning something as important as that to him.

Colour rushed to her cheeks. 'Oh, sorry! I didn't mean to leave that lying around.' She walked over and took the card from his hand, leaning against the worktop next to him and enveloping him in her familiar floral scent. She tapped the corner of the card gently against her palm and he watched, hypnotised by the action. 'It was on Wednesday. As you were away I didn't think it was worth mentioning.' She looked up at him from under her lashes. 'Don't worry—I didn't have a wild house party here while you were away, only a couple of friends over for dinner and we made sure to tidy up afterwards.'

Fighting a strange disquiet, he flapped a dismissive hand at her. 'Cara, it's okay for you to keep some of your things in the communal areas and have friends over for your birthday, for God's sake. I don't expect the place to be pristine the whole time.'

'Still. I meant to put this up in my room with the others.'

Despite their pact to be more open with each other, it was evidently going to take a lot more time and effort to get her to relax around him.

Maybe he should present her with some kind of peace offering. In fact, thinking about it, her birthday could provide the perfect excuse.

He'd seen her reading an article about a new play in a magazine one lunchtime last week, and when he picked it up later he noticed she'd put a ring around the box office number, as if to remind herself to book tickets.

After dispatching her back to the office with a list of clients to chase up about invoices, he called the theatre, only to find the play had sold out weeks ago. Not prepared to be defeated that easily, he placed a call to his friend James, who was a long-time benefactor of the theatre.

'Hey, man, how are things?' his friend asked as soon as he picked up.

'Great. Business is booming. How about you?'

'Life's good. Penny's pregnant again,' James said with pleasure in his voice.

Max ignored the twinge of pain in his chest. 'That's great. Congratulations.'

'Thanks. Let's just hope this one's going to give us less trouble arriving into the world.'

'You're certainly owed an easy birth after the last time.'

'You could say that. Anyway, what can I do for you, my friend?'

'I wanted to get hold of tickets for that new play at the Apollo Theatre for tonight's performance. It's my PA's birthday and I wanted to treat her, but it's sold out. Can you help me with that?'

'Your PA, huh?' There was a twist of wryness in James's voice that shot a prickle straight up his spine.

'Yeah. My PA,' he repeated with added terseness born of discomfort.

His friend chuckled. 'No problem. I'll call and get them to put some tickets aside for you for the VIP box. I saw it last week—it's great—but it starts early, at five, so you'll need to get a move on.' There was a loaded pause. 'It's good to hear you're getting out again.'

Max bristled again. 'I go out.'

'But not with women. Not since Jemima passed away.'

He sighed, beginning to wish he hadn't called now. 'It's not a date. She's my *PA*.'

James chuckled again. 'Well, she's lucky to have you for an *employer*. These tickets are like gold dust.'

'Thanks, I owe you one,' Max said, fighting hard to keep the growl out of his voice. To his annoyance, he felt rattled by what his friend was insinuating. It wasn't stepping over the line to do something like this for Cara, was it?

'Don't worry about it,' James said.

Max wasn't sure for a moment whether he'd voiced his concerns out loud and James was answering that question or whether he was just talking about paying him back the favour.

'Thanks, James, I've got to go,' he muttered, wanting to end the call so he could walk around and loosen off this weird tension in his chest.

'No worries.'

Max put the phone down, wondering again whether this gesture was a step too far.

No. She'd worked hard for him, under some testing circumstances and he wanted her to know that he appreciated it. If he wanted to retain her services—and he was pretty sure now that he did—he was going to have to make sure she knew how much she was valued here so she didn't go looking for another job.

Cara was back at her desk, busily typing away on her laptop, when he walked into the room they used as an office. Leaning against the edge of her desk, he waited until she'd finished and turned to face him.

'I'm nearly done here,' she said, only holding eye contact for a moment before glancing back at her computer.

'Great, because a friend of mine just called to say he has two spare tickets to that new play at the Apollo and I was thinking I could take you as a thank you for holding the fort so effectively whilst I've been away. And for missing your birthday.'

She stared at him as if she thought she might have misheard. 'I'm sorry?'

He smiled at her baffled expression, feeling a kink of pleasure at her reaction. 'We'll need to leave in the next few minutes if we're going to make it into town in time to catch the beginning.' He stood up and she blinked in surprise.

'You and *me*? Right *now*?'

'Yes. You don't have other plans, do you?'

'Um, no.'

He nodded. 'Great.'

Gesturing up and down her body, she frowned, looking a little flustered. 'But I can't go dressed like this.'

He glanced at her jeans and T-shirt, trying not to let his eyes linger on the way they fitted her trim, slender body. 'You're going to have to change quickly then,' he said, pulling his mobile out of his pocket and dialling the number for the taxi.

Cara chattered away in the cab all the way there about how the play had been given rave reviews after its preview performance and how people were already paying crazy money on auction websites for re-sold tickets to see it. Her enthusiasm was contagious and, stepping out of the car, he was surprised to find he was actually looking forward to seeing it.

The theatre was a recently renovated grand art deco building slap-bang in the middle of Soho, a short stroll from the hectic retail circus of Oxford Street.

It had been a while since he'd made it into town on a Friday night and even longer since he'd been to see any kind of live show. When he and Jemima had moved to London they'd been full of enthusiasm about how they'd be living in the heart of the action and would be able to go out every other night to see the most cutting-edge performances and mind-expanding lectures. They were going to become paragons of good taste and spectacularly cultured to boot.

And then real life had taken over and they'd become increasingly buried under the weight of work stress and life tiredness as the years went by and had barely made it out to anything at all. It had been fine when they'd had each other for company, but he was aware that he needed to make more of an effort to get out and be sociable now he was on his own.

Not that he'd been a total recluse since Jem had died; he'd been out with friends—Poppy being his most regular pub partner—but he'd done it in a cocoon of grief, always feeling slightly detached from what was going on around him.

Doing this with Cara meant he was having to make an effort again. Which was a good thing. It felt healthy. Perhaps that was why he was feeling more upbeat than he had in a while—as if there was life beyond the narrow world he'd been living in for the past year and a half.

After paying the taxi driver, they jogged straight to the box office for their tickets, then through the empty lobby to the auditorium to find their seats in the VIP box, the usher giving them a pointed look as she closed the doors firmly behind them. It seemed they'd only just made it. This theory was borne out by the dimming of the lights and the grand swish of the curtain opening just as they folded themselves into their seats.

Max turned to find Cara with her mouth comically open and an expression that clearly said *I can't believe we've just casually nipped into the best seats in the house.* He flashed her a quick smile, enjoying her pleasure and the sense of satisfaction at doing something good here, before settling back into his plush red velvet chair, his heart beating heavily in his chest.

A waft of her perfume hit his nose as she reached up to adjust her ponytail, which made his heart beat even harder—perhaps from the sudden sensory overload. Taking a deep breath, he concentrated on bringing his breathing back to normal and focused on the action on stage, determined to put all other thoughts aside for the meantime and try to enjoy whatever this turned out to be.

Cara was immensely relieved when the play stood up to her enthusiastic anticipation. It would have been pretty embarrassing if it had been a real flop after all the fuss she'd made about it on the way there. Every time she heard Max chuckle at one of the jokes she experienced a warm flutter of pleasure in her stomach.

Max bringing her here to the theatre had thrown her for a complete loop. Even though he'd finally let her into his head last weekend, she'd expected him to go back to being distant with her again once he came back from Manchester. But instead he'd surprised her by complimenting her, then not only getting tickets to the hottest play in London, but bringing her here himself as a reward for working hard.

Dumbfounded was not the word.

Not that she was complaining.

Sneaking a glance at him, she thought she'd never seen him looking so relaxed. She could hardly believe he was the same man who had opened the door to her on the first day they'd met. He seemed larger now somehow, as if he'd straightened up and filled out in the time since she'd last seen him. That had to be all in her head, of course, but he certainly seemed more *real* now that she knew what drove his rage. In fact it was incredible how differently she felt now she knew what sort of horror he'd been through—losing someone he loved in such a senseless way.

No wonder he was so angry at the world.

Selfishly, it was a massive relief to know that none of his dark moods had been about her performance—apart from when she'd fallen asleep on the kitchen table during business hours, of course.

After he'd left for Manchester, she'd had a minor panic attack about how she was going to cope on her own, terrified of making a mistake that would impact negatively on the business, but, after giving herself a good talking-to in the mirror, she'd pulled it together and got on with the job in hand. And she'd been fine. More than fine. In fact she'd actually started to enjoy her job again as she relaxed into the role and reasserted her working practices.

Truth be told, before she'd started working for Max, she didn't know whether she'd be able to hold her nerve in a business environment any more. He'd been a hard taskmaster but she knew she'd benefited from that, discovering that she had the strength to stand up for herself when it counted. She'd been tested to her limits and she'd come through the other side and that, to her, had been her biggest achievement in a very long time.

She felt proud of herself again.

As the first half drew to a close she became increasingly conscious of the heat radiating from Max's powerful body and his arm that pressed up against hers as he leaned into the armrest. Her skin felt hot and prickly where it touched his, as if he was giving off an electric charge, and it was sending little currents of energy through the most disconcerting places in her body.

It seemed her crush on him had grown right along with her respect and she was agonisingly aware of how easy it would be to fall for him if she let herself.

Which she wasn't going to do. He was clearly still in love with his wife and there was no way she could compete with a ghost.

Only pain and heartache lay that way.

As soon as the curtain swished closed and the lights came on to signal the intermission she sprang up from her seat, eager to break their physical connection as soon as possible.

'Let's grab a drink,' Max said, leaning in close so she could hear him over the noise of audience chatter, his breath tickling the hairs around her ear.

'Good idea.' She was eager to move now to release the pent-up energy that was making her heart race.

Max gestured for her to go first, staying close behind her as they walked down the stairs towards the bar, his dominating presence like a looming shadow at her back.

They joined the rest of the audience at the bottom of the stairs and she pushed her way through the shouty crowd of people towards the shiny black-lacquered bar, which was already six people deep with waiting customers.

'Hmm, this could take a while,' she said to Max as they came to a stop at the outskirts of the throng.

'Don't worry, I'll get the drinks,' he said, walking around the perimeter of the group as if gauging the best place to make a start. 'Glass of wine?' he asked.

'Red please.'

'Okay, I'm going in,' he said, taking an audible breath and turning to the side to shoulder through a small gap between two groups of chatting people with their backs to each other.

Cara watched in fascinated awe as Max made it to the bar in record time, flipping a friendly smile as he sidled through the crowd and charming a group of women into letting him into a small gap at the counter next to them.

After making sure his newly made friends were served first, he placed his order with the barman and was back a few moments later, two glasses of red wine held aloft in a gesture of celebration.

'Wow, nice work,' Cara said, accepting a glass and trying not to grin like a loon. 'I've never seen anyone work a bar crowd like that before.'

Max shrugged and took a sip of wine, pinning a look of exaggerated nonchalance onto his face. 'I have hidden depths.'

She started to laugh, but it dried in her throat as she locked eyes with someone on the other side of the room.

Someone she thought she'd never see again.

Swallowing hard, she dragged her gaze back to Max and dredged up a smile, grasping for cool so she wouldn't have to explain her sudden change in mood.

But it was not to be. The man was too astute for his own good.

'Are you okay? You look like you've seen
a ghost,' he said, his intelligent eyes flashing
with concern.

Damn and blast. This was the last thing she
wanted to have to deal with tonight.

'Fine,' she squeaked, her cheeks growing
hot under the intensity of his gaze.

'Cara. I thought we'd agreed to be straight
with each other from now on.'

Sighing, she nodded towards the other
side of the bar. 'That guy over there is an old
friend of mine.'

He frowned as she failed to keep the hurt
out of her voice and she internally kicked herself for being so transparent.

'He can't be a very good friend if you're
ignoring each other.'

She sighed and tapped at the floor with the
toe of her shoe. 'It's complicated.'

He raised his eyebrows, waiting for her to
go on.

After pausing for a moment, she decided
there was no point in trying to gloss over
it. 'The thing is—his fiancée has a problem
with me.'

'Really? Why?'

'Because I'm female.'

He folded his arms. 'She's the jealous type, huh?'

'Yeah. And no matter how much Jack's tried to convince her that our friendship is purely platonic, she won't believe him. So I've been confined to the rubbish heap of Friends Lost and Passed Over.' She huffed out a sigh. 'I can't really blame him for making that choice, though. He loves her and I want him to be happy, and if that means we can't be friends any more then so be it.'

The look of bewildered outrage in Max's expression made the breath catch in her throat and she practically stopped breathing altogether as he reached out and stroked his hand down her arm in a show of solidarity, his touch sending tingles of pure pleasure through every nerve in her body.

Staring up into his handsome face, she wondered again what it would feel like to have someone like Max for a partner. To know that he was on her side and that he had her back, no matter what happened.

But she was kidding herself. He was never going to offer her the chance to find out. She was his employee and she'd do well to remember that.

Tearing her gaze away from him, she glanced back across the room to where the fiancée in question had now appeared by Jack's side. From a distance they appeared to be having a heated discussion about something, their heads close together as they gesticulated at each other. As she watched, they suddenly sprang apart and Jack turned to catch her eye again, already moving towards where she and Max were standing.

He was coming over.

Her body tensed with apprehension and she jumped in surprise as Max put his hand on her arm again, then increased his grip, as if readying himself to spirit her away from a painful confrontation.

'Cara! It's been ages,' Jack said as he came to a stop in front of her, looking just as boyishly handsome as ever, with his lopsided grin and great mop of wavy blond hair.

'It has, Jack.'

'How are you?' he asked, looking a little shame-faced now, as well he should. They'd become good friends after meeting at their first jobs after university and had been close once, spending weekends at each other's houses and standing in as 'plus ones' at weddings and parties if either of them were single and in need of support.

There had been a time when she'd wondered whether they'd end up together, but as time had passed it became obvious that wasn't meant to be. He was a great guy, but the chemistry just wasn't there for her—or for him, it seemed. But seeing him here now reminded her just how much she missed his friendship. She could have really done with his support after Ewan sauntered away from their relationship in search of someone with less emotional baggage, but it had been at that point that his fiancée had issued her ultimatum, and Cara had well and truly been the loser in that contest.

Not that she blamed him for choosing Amber. She had to respect his loyalty to the woman he loved.

'I'm great, Jack, thanks. How are you—' she paused and flicked her gaze to his fiancée, who had now appeared at his side '—both?' Somehow she managed to dredge up a smile for the woman. 'Hi, Amber.'

'Hi, Cara, we're great, thanks,' Amber said,

acerbity dripping from every word as she pointedly wrapped a possessive arm around Jack's waist. Turning to look at Max, she gave him a subtle, but telling, once-over.

'And who's this?'

'This is Max…' Cara took a breath, about to say *my boss*, when Max cut her off to lean in and shake hands with Amber.

'It's lovely to meet you, Amber,' he said in the same smooth tone she'd heard him use to appease clients.

It worked just as well on Amber because her cheeks flooded with colour and she actually fluttered her lashes at him. Turning back to Cara, she gave her a cool smile, her expression puzzled, as if she was trying to work out how she'd got her hands on someone as impressive as Max.

'Did Jack tell you—our wedding's on Sunday so this evening is our last hurrah before married life?' Amber's eyes twinkled with malice. 'Jack's firm is very well reputed in the City and people practically throw invitations at him every day,' she said, her tone breezy but her eyes hard, as though she was challenging Cara to beat her with something better than that.

Which, of course, she had no hope of doing.

Pushing away the thump of humiliation, Cara forced her mouth into the shape of a smile.

'That's wonderful—congratulations! I had no idea the wedding was so soon.'

Amber leaned in and gave her a pitying smile. 'We've kept it a small affair, which is why we couldn't send you an invitation, Cara.'

Max shifted next to her, pulling her a bit tighter against him in the process and surprising her again by rubbing her arm in support. She wondered whether he could feel how fast her pulse was racing through her body with him holding her so close.

'But we had two spaces open up this week,' Jack said suddenly and a little too loudly, as if he'd finally decided to step out of his fiancée's shadow and take control. 'My cousin and her husband have had to drop out to visit sick family abroad. If you're not busy you could come in their place.'

Judging by the look on Amber's face, she obviously hadn't had this in mind when she'd agreed to be dragged over here.

'It would be great if you could make it,'

Jack pressed, his expression open, almost pleading now. It seemed that he genuinely wanted her to be there. Perhaps this was his way of making things up to her after cutting her out of his life so brutally. At least that was something.

But she couldn't say yes when the invitation was for both her and Max and she hated the idea of turning up and spending the day on her own amongst all those happy couples.

Before she could open her mouth to make up an excuse and turn them down, Max leaned in and said, 'Thank you—we'd love to come.'

She swivelled her head to gape at him, almost giving herself whiplash in the process, stunned to find a look of cool certainty on his face.

'Are you sure we're not busy?' she said pointedly, raising both eyebrows at him.

'I'm sure,' he replied with a firm nod.

Turning back to Jack, she gave him what must have been the weirdest-looking smile. 'Okay—er—' she swallowed '—then we'd love to come. Thanks.'

'That's great,' Jack said, giving her a look

that both said *I'm sorry for everything* and *thank you*.

'We'd better go and get a drink before the performance starts again,' Amber said with steel in her voice, her patience clearly used up now.

'I'll text you with the details, Cara,' Jack said as Amber drew him away.

'Okay, see you on Sunday,' Cara said weakly to their disappearing figures.

As soon as they were out of earshot she turned to stare at Max, no doubt doing her impression of a goldfish again.

'He's a brave man,' was all Max said in reply.

'You realise they think we're a couple?'

He nodded, a fierce intensity in his eyes causing a delicious shiver to rush down her spine. 'I know, but I wanted to see the look on that awful woman's face when we said yes, and I have no problem pretending to be your partner if it's going to smooth the way back to a friendship with Jack for you.'

Max as her partner. Just the thought of it made her quiver right down to her toes.

'That's—' she searched for the right words '—game of you.'

'It'll be my pleasure.'

There was an odd moment where the noises around her seemed to get very loud in her ears. Tearing her gaze away from his, she gulped down the last of her wine and wrapped her hands around the glass in order to prevent herself from chewing on her nails.

Okay. Well, that happened.

Who knew that Max would turn out to be her knight in shining armour?

CHAPTER SIX

MAX HAD NO idea where this strange posses-
siveness towards Cara had sprung from, but
he hadn't been about to let that awful woman,
Amber, treat her with so little respect. She
deserved more than that. Much more. And
while she was working for him he was going
to make sure she got it.

Which meant he was now going to be es-
corting her to a wedding—the kind of event
he'd sworn to avoid after Jemima died. The
thought of being back in a church, watching
a couple with their whole lives ahead of them
begin their journey together, made his stomach clench with unease.

One year—that was all he'd been allowed
with his wife. One lousy year. It made him
want to spit with rage at the world. Why her?
Why them?

Still, at least he didn't know the happy couple and would be able to keep a low profile at the wedding, hiding his bitterness behind a bland smile. He didn't need to engage. He'd just be there to support Cara; that was all.

After the play finished they travelled home in silence, a stark contrast to their journey there, but he was glad of the quiet. Perversely, it felt as though he and Cara had grown closer during that short time, the confrontation and subsequent solidarity banding them together like teammates.

Which of course they were, he reminded himself as he opened the front door to his house and ushered her inside, at least when it came to the business.

Cara's phone beeped as she shrugged off her coat and she plucked it out of her handbag and read the message, her smile dropping by degrees as she scanned the text.

'Problem?' he asked, an uncomfortable sense of foreboding pricking at the edge of his mind. It had taken him a long time to be able to answer the phone without feeling the crush of anxiety he'd been plagued with after the call telling him his wife had collapsed and had been rushed into hospital.

He took a step closer to her, glad she was

here to distract him from the lingering bad memories.

Glancing up, she gave him a sheepish look. 'It's a text from Jack with the details of the wedding.'

'Oh, right.' He stepped back, relief flowing through him, but Cara didn't appear to relax. Instead her grimace only deepened.

'Um. Apparently it's in Leicestershire. Which is a two and a half hour drive from here. So we'll need to stay overnight.' She wrinkled her nose, the apology clear on her face.

Great. Just what had he let himself in for here?

'No problem,' he forced himself to say, holding back the irritation he felt at the news. It wasn't Cara's fault and he was the one who had pushed for this to happen.

More fool him.

'Really? You don't mind?' she asked, relief clear in her tone.

'No, it's fine,' he lied, trying not to think about all the hours he'd have to spend away from his desk so he could make nice with a bunch of strangers.

'Great, then I'll book us a couple of rooms

in the B&B that Jack suggested,' she said, her smile returning.

'You do that.' He gave her a firm nod and hid a yawn behind his hand. 'I'm heading off to bed,' he said, feeling the stress of the week finally catching up with him. 'See you in the morning, Cara. And Happy Birthday.'

Cara disappeared for most of the next day, apparently going to look at potential flats to rent, then retiring to bed early, citing exhaustion from the busy, but fruitless, day.

After the tension of Friday night, Max was glad of the respite and spent most of his time working through the backlog of emails he'd accumulated after his week away.

Sunday finally rolled around and he woke early, staring into the cool empty air next to him and experiencing the usual ache of hollowness in his chest, before pulling himself together and hoisting his carcass out of bed and straight into the shower.

The wedding was at midday so at least he had a couple of hours to psych himself up before they had to head over to the Leicestershire estate where it was being held.

The sun was out and glinting off the polished windows of the houses opposite when he pulled his curtains open, momentarily blinding him with its brightness. It was definitely a day for being outdoors.

He'd barely breathed fresh air in the past week, only moving between office and hotel, and the thought of feeling the warm sun on his skin spurred him into action. He pulled on his running gear, something he'd not done for over a year and a half, and went for a long run, welcoming the numbing pain as he worked his lethargic muscles hard, followed by the rewarding rush of serotonin as it chased its way through his veins. After a while it felt as though he was flying along the pavement, the worries and stresses of the past week pushed to the very back of his mind by the punishing exercise.

For the first time in a long while he felt as if he were truly awake.

Cara appeared to be up and about when he limped back into his kitchen for a long drink of water, his senses perking up as he breathed in the comforting smell of the coffee she'd been drinking, threaded with the flowery scent of her perfume.

Glancing up at the clock as he knocked back

his second glass of water, he was shocked to see it was already nearly nine o'clock, which meant he really ought to get a move on if he was going to be ready to leave for the wedding on time.

Turning back from loading his glass into the dishwasher, he was brought up short by the sight of Cara standing in the hallway just outside the kitchen door, watching him. She'd twisted her long hair up into some sort of complicated-looking hairstyle and her dark eyes sparkled with glittery make-up. The elegant silver strapless dress she wore fitted her body perfectly, moulding itself to her gentle curves and making her seem taller and—something else. More mature, perhaps? More sophisticated?

Whatever it was, she looked completely and utterly beautiful.

Realising he was standing there gawping at her like some crass teenage boy, he cleared his suddenly dry throat and dredged up a smile which he hoped didn't look as lascivious as it felt.

'Hey, you look like you're dressed for a wedding,' he said, cringing inside at how pathetic that sounded.

She smiled. 'And you don't. I hope you're not thinking of going like that because I'm pretty sure it didn't say "sports casual" on the invitation.' Her amused gaze raked up and down his body, her eyebrows rising at the sight of his sweat-soaked running gear.

He returned her grin, finding it strangely difficult to keep it natural-looking. His whole face felt as if he'd had his head stuck in the freezer. What was wrong with him? A bit of sunshine and a fancy dress and his mind was in a spin.

'I'd better go and take a shower; otherwise we're going to be late,' he said, already walking towards the door.

'Could you do me a favour before you go?' she asked, colour rising in her cheeks.

'Er…sure. As long as it's not going to cost me anything,' he joked, coming to a stop in front of her. In her heels she was nearly as tall as him, making it easier to directly meet her gaze. She had such amazing eyes: bright and clear with vitality and intellect. The make-up and hair made him think of Audrey Hepburn in *Breakfast at Tiffany's*.

'Could you do up the buttons on the back of my dress?' she asked, her voice sounding unusually breathy, as if it had taken a lot for her to ask for his help.

'Sure,' he said, waiting for her to turn

around and present her back to him. His breath caught as he took in the long, elegant line of her spine as it disappeared into the base of her dress. There were three buttons that held the top half of it together, with a large piece cut out at the bottom, which would leave her creamy skin and the gentle swells of muscle at the base of her back exposed.

Heaven help him.

Hands feeling as if they'd been trapped in the freezer, too, he fiddled around with the buttons, feeling the warmth of her skin heat the tips of his fingers. Hot barbs of awareness tracked along his nerves and embedded themselves deep in his body and his breath came out in short ragged gasps, which he'd like to think was an after-effect of the hard exercise, but was more likely to be down to his close proximity to a woman's body, after his had been starved of attention for the past year and a half.

'There you go,' he said, snapping the final button into its hole with a sigh of relief. 'I'll be back down in fifteen.'

And with that he made his escape.

Wow. This felt weird, being at Jack's wedding—a friend she thought she'd never see again—with Max—her recalcitrant boss—as her escort. The whole world seemed to have flipped on its head. If someone had told her a week ago that this was going to happen she would have given them a polite smile whilst slowly backing away.

But here she was, swaying unsteadily in the only pair of high heels she owned, with Max at her side. The man who could give Hollywood's top leading men a run for their money in the charisma department.

There had been a moment in the kitchen, after he'd turned around and noticed her, when she thought she'd seen something in his eyes. Something that had never been there before. Something like desire.

And then when he'd helped her with her dress it had felt as though the air had crackled and jumped between them. The bloom of his breath on her neck had made her knees weak and her heart race. She could have sworn his voice had held a rougher undertone than she was used to hearing as he excused himself.

But she knew she was kidding herself if she thought she should read more than friendly interest into his actions.

They had Radio Four on for the entire journey up to Leicestershire, listening in rapt silence to a segment on finance, then chuckling along to a radio play. Cara was surprised by how easy it was to sit beside Max and how relaxed and drawn into their shared enjoyment of the programme she was. So much so, that it was to her great surprise that they pulled into the small car park of the church where the wedding was taking place, seemingly only a short time after leaving London.

The sunshine that had poured in through her bedroom window that morning had decided to stick around for the rest of the day, disposing of the insubstantial candyfloss clouds of the morning to reveal the most intensely blue sky she'd ever seen.

All around her, newly blooming spring flowers bopped their heads in time to the rhythm of the light spring breeze, their gaudy colours a striking counterpoint to the verdant green of the lawns surrounding them.

Taking a deep breath, she drew the sweet, fresh air deep into her lungs. This should mark a new beginning in her life, she decided. The start of the next chapter, where the foundations she'd laid in the past few weeks would hopefully prove strong enough to support her from this point onwards.

'It's nearly twelve o'clock; we should go in,' Max said with regret in his voice as he cast his gaze around their beautiful surroundings.

Attempting to keep her eyes up and off the tantalising view of his rear in the well-cut designer suit he'd chosen to wear today, she tripped into the church after him, shivering slightly at the change in temperature as they walked out of the sunshine and into the nave.

Most of the pews were already full, so they hung back for a moment to be directed to a seat by one of the ushers.

And that was when the day took a definite turn for the worse.

Her world seemed to spin on its axis, rolling her stomach along with it, as her former and current life lined up on a collision course. One of the PAs who had belonged to the Cobra Clique was standing down by the altar, her long blond hair slithering down her back as she threw her head back and laughed at something that the man standing next to her said.

Taking a deep breath, Cara willed herself not to panic, but her distress must have shown plainly on her face because Max turned to glance in the direction she was staring and said, 'Cara? What's wrong?'

'Ah…nothing.' She flapped a dismissive hand at him, feeling her cheeks flame with heat, and took a step backwards, hoping the stone pillar would shield her. But serendipity refused to smile as the woman turned towards them, catching her eye, her pupils flaring in recognition and her gaze moving, as if in slow motion, from Cara to Max and back again. And the look on her face plainly said she wasn't going to miss this golden opportunity to make more trouble for her.

Looking around her wildly, Cara's heart sank as she realised there was nowhere to run, nowhere to hide.

It was usually at this point in a film that the leading lady would pull the guy she was with towards her and kiss him hard to distract him from the oncoming danger, but she knew, as she stared with regret at Max's full, inviting mouth, that there was no way she could do that. He'd probably choke in shock, then fire her on the spot if she even attempted it. It wouldn't just put her job in jeopardy—it would blow it to smithereens.

There was only one thing left to do.

'Max, I need to tell you something.'

He frowned at her, his eyes darkening as he caught on to her worried tone.

'What's wrong?'

'I—er—'

'Cara?' He looked really alarmed now and she shook her head, trying to clear it. She needed to keep her cool or she'd end up looking even more of an idiot.

'I wasn't entirely straight with you about why I left my last job. Truth is—' she took a breath '—I didn't take redundancy.'

He blinked, then frowned. 'So you were fired?'

'No. I—'

'What did you do, Cara? What are you trying to tell me?' His voice held a tinge of the old Max now—the one who didn't suffer fools.

'Okay—' She closed her eyes and held up a hand. 'Look, just give me a minute and I'll explain. The thing is—' Locking her shaking hands together, she took a steadying breath. 'I was bullied by a gang of women there who made my life a living hell and I handed in my notice before my boss could fire me for incompetence as a result of it,' she said, mortified by the tremor in her voice.

When she opened her eyes to look at him, the expression of angry disbelief on his face made her want to melt into a puddle of shame.

'What?'

She swallowed past the tightness in her throat. 'I had no choice but to leave.'

He shook his head in confusion. 'Why didn't you tell me?'

Out of the corner of her eye she saw her nemesis approaching and felt every hair on her body stand to attention. The woman was only ten steps away, at most.

'And why are you telling me this now?' he pressed.

'Because one of the women is here at the wedding and she'll probably tell you a pack of lies to make me look bad. I didn't exactly leave graciously. There was a jug of cold coffee and some very white blouses involved.' She cringed at the desperation in her voice, but Max just turned to glare in the direction she'd been avoiding, then let out a sharp huff of breath.

'Come outside for a minute.'

Wrapping his hand around her arm, he propelled her back out through the doors of the church and down the steps, coming to a sudden halt under the looming shadow of the clock tower, where he released her. Crossing his arms, he looked down at her with an expression of such exasperation it made her quake in her stilettos.

'Why didn't you mention this to me before?' he asked, shoving back the hair that had fallen across his forehead during their short journey, only drawing more attention to his piercing gaze.

Sticking her chin in the air, she crossed her own arms, determined to stand up for herself. 'I really wanted to work with you and I thought you might not hire me if you knew the truth. It didn't exactly look good on my CV that I'd only stuck it out there for three months before admitting defeat.'

'So you thought you had to lie to me to get the job?'

She held up her hands in apology. 'I know I should have told you the truth, but I'd already messed up other job interviews because I was so nervous and ashamed of myself for being so weak.' She hugged her arms around her again. 'I didn't want you to think badly of me.

Anyway, at the time you barely wanted to talk to me about the work I had to do, let alone anything of a personal nature, so I thought it best to keep it to myself.' She looked at him steadily, craving his understanding. 'You can be pretty intimidating, you know.'

She was saved from having to further explain herself by one of the ushers loudly asking the stragglers outside to please go into the church and take their seats because the bride had arrived.

From the look on Max's face she wasn't sure whether he was going to walk away and leave her standing there like a total lemon on her own or turn around and punch the wall. She didn't fancy watching either scenario play out.

To her surprise, he let out a long, frustrated sigh and looked towards the gaggle of people filing into the church.

'We can't talk about this now or we'll be walking in with the bridal party, and there's no way I'd pass for a bridesmaid,' he said stiffly.

She stared at him. 'You mean you're not going to leave?'

'No, I'm not going to leave,' he said crossly. 'We'll talk more about this after the ceremony.'

And with that he put his hand firmly against the middle of her back and ushered her inside.

Sliding into the polished wooden pew next to Max and surreptitiously wiping her damp palms on her dress, she glanced at him out of the corner of her eye. From the set of his shoulders she could tell he wasn't likely to let *this* go with a casual wave of his hand.

In fact she'd bet everything she had left that he was really going to fire her this time.

Frustration churned in her stomach. After all the progress she'd made in getting back on her feet, and persuading Max to finally trust her, was it really going to end like this?

Looking along the pews, she saw that her nemesis was sitting on the other side of the church, a wide smile on her face as she watched the ceremony unfold. At least that threat had been neutralised. There wasn't anything left that she could do to hurt her.

She hoped.

Rage unfurled within Cara at the unfairness of it all. Why did this woman get to enjoy herself when she had to sit here worrying about her future?

As she watched Amber make her stately way up the aisle towards a rather nervous-looking Jack, she could barely concentrate for wondering what Max was going to say to her once they were facing each other over their garlic mushrooms at the lunch afterwards. There was no way she was going to be able to force down a bite of food until they'd resolved this.

Oh, get a grip, Cara.

When she dared take a peek at him from the corner of her eye again, he seemed to be grimly staring straight ahead. Forcing herself to relax, she uncrossed her legs, then her arms and sat up straighter, determined not to appear anxious or pitiful. She knew what she had to do. There would be no gratuitous begging or bartering for a reprieve. She would hold her head high throughout it all and calmly state her case.

And until she had that opportunity she was going to damn well enjoy watching her friend get married.

Judging by her rigid posture and ashen complexion, Cara really didn't appear to be enjoying the ceremony, which only increased Max's discomfort at being there, too. Not that he blamed her in any way for it. He'd chosen to come here with her after all. Though, from the sound of it, she must be regretting bringing him along now.

Had he really been so unapproachable that she'd chosen to lie to his face instead of admitting to having a rough time at her last place of work?

He sighed inwardly.

She was absolutely right, though. Again. He could be intimidating. And he'd been at the peak of his remoteness when she'd first arrived on his doorstep and asked him for a job. He also knew that if she'd mentioned the personal issues that had been intrinsic to her leaving her last job when they'd first met it would have given him pause enough to turn her away. He hadn't wanted any kind of complication at that point.

But he was so glad now that he hadn't.

Somehow, in her innocent passive-aggressive way, she'd managed to push his buttons and, even though he'd fought it at the time, that was exactly what he'd needed.

She was what he'd needed.

After the ceremony finished they were immediately ushered out of the church and straight up the sweeping manicured driveway to the front of a grand Georgian house where an enormous canvas marquee had been set up next to the orangery.

A small affair, his foot.

As soon as they stepped inside they had toxic-coloured cocktails thrust upon them and were politely but firmly asked to make their way back outside again to the linen-draped tables on the terrace next to the house.

'This is like a military operation,' he muttered to Cara, who had walked quietly next to him since they'd left the church, her face pale and her expression serious. She gave him a weak smile, her eyes darting from side to side as if she was seriously contemplating making a run for it and scoping out the best means of escape.

He sighed. 'Come and sit down over here where it's quiet,' he said, looping his arm through hers and guiding her towards one of the empty tables nearest the house.

To his frustration she stiffened, then slipped out of his steadying grip and folded her arms across her chest instead, her shoulders rigid and her chin firmly up as they walked. Just as they picked their way over the last bit of gravelled path to reach the table she stumbled and on reflex he quickly moved in to catch her.

'Are you okay?' he asked, placing a hand on the exposed part of her back, feeling the heat of her body warm the palm of his hand and send an echoing sensation through his entire abdomen.

His touch seemed to undo something in her and she collapsed into the nearest chair and gave him such a fearful look his heart jumped into his throat.

'I'm sorry for lying to you, Max. Please don't fire me. If I lose this job I'll have to move back to Cornwall and I really, really don't want to leave London. It's my home and I love it. I can't imagine living anywhere else now. And I really like working for you.' Swallowing hard, she gave him a small quavering smile. 'I swear I will never lie to you again. Believe it or not, I usually have a rock-solid moral compass and if I hadn't felt backed into a corner I never would have twisted the truth. I was on the cusp of losing everything and I was desperate, Max. Totally. Desperate.' She punctuated each of the last words with a slap of her hand on the table.

'Cara, I'm not going to fire you.'

How could she think that he would? Good grief, had he done such a number on her that she'd think he'd be capable of something as heartless as that?

'You're not?' Her eyes shone in the reflected brightness thrown up by the white tablecloth and he looked away while she blinked back threatening tears.

'Of course not.' He shifted forward in his seat, closer to her. 'You well and truly proved your worth to the business last week.' He waited till she looked at him again. 'I have to admit, I'm hurt that you thought I'd fire you for admitting to being bullied.' He leaned back in his chair with a sigh. 'God, you must think I'm a real tool if you seriously believed I'd do something like that.'

'It's just—you can be a bit…fierce…sometimes. And I didn't want to show any weakness.' She visibly cringed as she said it, and his insides plummeted.

'Tell me more about what happened at your last job,' he said quietly, wanting to get things completely straight between them, but not wanting to spook her further in the process.

Her gaze slid away. 'It's not a happy tale, or something I'm particularly proud of.'

'No. I got that impression.'

'Okay, I'll tell you, but please don't judge me too harshly. Things like this always look so simple and manageable from a distance, but when you're in the thick of it, it's incredibly difficult to think straight without letting your emotions get in the way.'

He held up his hands, palms forward, and affected a non-judgemental expression.

She nodded and sat up straighter. 'I thought I'd hit the jackpot when I was offered that position. Ugh! What an idiot,' she said, her self-conscious grimace making him want to move closer to her, to draw her towards him and smooth out the kinks of her pain. But he couldn't do that. It wasn't his place.

So he just nodded and waited for her to continue.

'When I started as Executive Assistant to the CEO of LED Software I had no idea about the office politics that were going on there. But it didn't take me long to find out. Apparently one of the other PAs had expected to be a shoo-in for my job and was *very* unimpressed when they gave it to me. She made it her mission from my first day to make my life miserable. As one of the longest-standing members of staff—and a very, er, *strong* personality—she had the allegiance of all the other PAs and a lot of the other members of staff and they ganged up on me. At first I thought I was going mad. I'd make diary appointments for my boss with other high-ranking members of staff in the company, which their PAs would claim to have no knowledge of by the time I sent him along for the meeting. Or the notes I'd print out for an important phone call with the Executive Board would go missing from his desk right before it took place and he'd have to take it unbriefed.' She tapped her fingers on the table. 'That did not go down well. My boss was a very proud guy and he expected things to be perfect.'

'I can relate to that,' Max said, forcing compassion into his smile despite the tug of disquiet in his gut. He was just as guilty when it came to perfectionism.

But, instead of admonishing him, she smiled back.

'Lots of other little things like that happened,' she continued, rubbing a hand across her forehead, 'which made me look incompetent, but I couldn't prove that someone was interfering with my work and when I mentioned it to my boss he'd wave away my concerns and suggest I was slipping up on the job and blaming others to cover my back. I let the stress of it get to me and started making real mistakes, things I never would have let slip at the last place I worked. It rattled me, to the point where I started believing I wasn't cut out for the job. I wasn't sleeping properly with the stress of it and I ended up breaking down one day in front of my boss. And that—' she clicked her fingers '—was the end of our working relationship. He seemed to lose all respect for me after that and started giving the other PAs things that were my job to do.'

Max snorted in frustration. 'The guy sounds like an idiot.'

She gave him a wan smile. 'I was the idiot. I only found out what was really going on when I overheard a couple of the PAs laughing about it in the ladies' bathroom.'

Her eyes were dark with an expression he couldn't quite read now. Was it anger? Resentment? It certainly didn't look like self-pity.

'So you left,' he prompted.

She took a sip of her drink and he did the

same, grimacing at the claggy sweetness of the cocktail.

'I had to,' she said. 'My professional reputation was at stake, not to mention my sanity. I couldn't afford to be fired; it would have looked awful on my CV. Not to mention how upset my parents would have been. They're desperate for me to have a successful career. They never had the opportunity to get a good education or well-paid job themselves so they scrimped and saved for years to put me through private school. It's a point of pride for my dad in particular. Apparently he never shuts up to his friends about me working with "the movers and shakers in the Big Smoke".' She shot him an embarrassed grimace.

He smiled. 'You're lucky—my mother couldn't give two hoots whether I'm successful or not. She's not what you'd call an engaged parent.'

Her brow furrowed in sympathy. 'And your father?'

'I never met him.' He leant back with a sigh. 'My mother fell pregnant with me when she was sixteen and still maintains that she doesn't know who he was. She was pretty wild in her youth and constantly moved us around the country. Barely a term at school would go by before she had us packing up and moving on. She couldn't bear to stay in the same place for long. Not that she's exactly settled now.'

Her gaze was sympathetic. 'That must have been tough when you were young.'

He shrugged. 'It was a bit. I never got to keep the friends I made for very long.'

He thought about how his unsettled youth had impacted on the way he liked to live now. He still didn't like change, even all these years later; it made him tetchy and short-tempered. Which was something Cara had got to know all about recently.

Keen to pull his mind away from his own shortcomings, he leaned forward in his seat and recaptured eye contact with her. 'So what happened when you handed in your notice?'

She started at the sudden flip in subject back to her and twisted the stem of her glass in her fingers, looking away from his gaze and focusing on the garish liquid as it swirled up towards the rim. 'My boss didn't even bat an eyelid, just tossed my letter of resignation onto his desk and went back to the email he was typing, which confirmed just how insignificant I was to him. I took a couple of weeks to get my head straight after that, but I needed another job. I've never earned enough to build up any savings and my landlord chose that moment to hoick my rent up. I sent my CV out everywhere and got a few interviews, but every one I attended was a washout. It was as if they could sense the cloud of failure that hung around me like a bad smell.'

'And that's when Poppy sent you to me.'

Wrinkling her nose, she gave him a rueful smile. 'I told her a bit about what had happened before she went off to shoot her latest project and she must have thought the two of us could help each other out because she emailed me to suggest I try you for a job. She made it sound as if you were desperate for help and it seemed like fate that I should work for you.'

'Desperate, huh?' He leant back in his seat and raised an eyebrow, feeling amusement tug at his mouth. That was textbook Poppy. 'Well, I have to admit it's been good for me, having you around. It's certainly kept me on my toes.'

'Yeah, there's never a dull moment when I'm around, huh?'

The air seemed to grow thick between them as their eyes met and he watched in arrested fascination as her cheeks flamed with colour.

Sliding her gaze away, she stared down at the table, clutching her glass, her chewed nails in plain view. He'd known it the whole time, of course, that she was fighting against some inner trauma, as her nerve and buoyancy deteriorated in the face of his brittle moods. Her increasingly ragged nails had been the indicator he'd been determined to ignore.

But not any more.

A string quartet suddenly started up on the terrace behind them and he winced as the sound assaulted his ears. He'd never liked the sound of violins and an instrument such as that should never be used to play soft rock covers. It was a crime against humanity.

'Come on, let's take a walk around the grounds and clear our heads,' he said, standing up and holding out his hand to help her up from the chair.

She looked at it with that little frown that always made something twist in his chest, before giving a firm nod and putting her hand in his.

CHAPTER SEVEN

A WALK WAS exactly what Cara needed to clear her head.

She couldn't quite believe she'd just spilled her guts to Max like that, but it was a massive relief to have it all out in the open, even if she did still feel shaky with the effort of holding herself together.

Of course, seeing the concern on his handsome face had only made her ridiculous crush on him deepen, and she was beginning to worry about how she was going to cope with seeing him every day, knowing that they'd never be anything more than colleagues or, at the very most, friends.

A twinkling light in the distance danced in her peripheral vision and she stopped and turned to see what it was, feeling her heels sink into the soft earth beneath her feet. Pulling her shoes off, she hooked her fingers into the straps before running to catch up with Max, who was now a few paces ahead of her, seemingly caught up in his own world, his head dipped as a frown played across his brow.

'Hey, do you fancy walking to that lake over there?' she asked him.

'Hmm?' His eyes looked unfocused, as if his thoughts were miles away. 'Yes, okay.'

The sudden detachment worried her. 'Is everything okay?' Perhaps, now he'd had more time to reflect on what she'd told him, he was starting to regret getting involved in her messed up life.

She took a breath. 'Do you want to head back to London? I wouldn't blame you if you did.'

Turning to look her in the eye again, he blinked, as though casting away whatever was bothering him. 'No, no. I'm fine.' His gaze flicked towards the lake, then back to her again and he gave her a tense smile. 'Yeah, let's walk that way.'

It only took them a couple of minutes to get there, now that she was in bare feet, and they stopped at the lakeshore and looked out across the water to the dark, impenetrable-looking forest on the other side.

'It's a beautiful setting they've chosen,' Cara said, to fill the heavy silence that had fallen between them.

'Yes, it's lovely.' Max bent down and picked up a smooth flat stone, running his fingertips across its surface. 'This looks like a good skimmer.' He shrugged off his jacket and rolled up the sleeves of his shirt, revealing his muscular forearms.

Cara stared at them, her mouth drying at the sight. There was something so real, so virile about the image of his tanned skin, with its smattering of dark hair, in stark contrast to the crisp white cotton of his formal shirt. As if he was revealing the *man* inside the businessman.

Supressing a powerful desire to reach out and trace her fingers across the dips and swells of his muscles, she took a step away to give him plenty of room as he drew his elbow back and bent low, then flung the stone hard across the water.

A deep, satisfied chuckle rumbled from his chest as the stone bounced three times across the still surface, spinning out rings of gentle ripples in its wake, before sinking without a trace into the middle of the lake.

He turned to face her with a grin, his eyes alive with glee, and she couldn't help but smile back.

'Impressive.'

He blew on his fingers and pretended to polish them on his shirt. 'I'm a natural. What can I say?'

Seeing his delight at the achievement, she had a strong desire to get in on the fun. Perhaps it would help distract her from thinking about how alone they were out here on the edge of the lake. 'Does your natural talent stretch to teaching me how to do that?'

'You've never skimmed a stone?' He looked so over-the-top incredulous she couldn't help but laugh.

'Never.'

'Didn't you say your parents live in Cornwall? Surely there's plenty of opportunities to be near water there.'

She snorted and took a step backwards, staring down at the muddy grass at their feet. 'Yeah, if you live near the coast, which they don't. I never learnt to drive when I was living there and my parents didn't take me to the beach that much when I was young. My dad's always suffered with a bad back from the heavy lifting he has to do at work, so he never got involved in anything of a physical nature. And my mum's a real homebody. She's suffered with agoraphobia for years.'

She heard him let out a low exhalation of breath and glanced up to find an expression of real sympathy in his eyes. 'I'm sorry to hear that. That must have been hard for you as a kid,' he said softly.

Shrugging one shoulder, she gave a nod to acknowledge his concern, remembering the feeling of being trapped inside four small walls when she was living at home, with nowhere to escape to. Going to school every day had actually been a welcome escape from it and as soon as she'd finished her studies she'd hightailed it to London.

'Yeah, it was a bit. My parents are good people, though. They threw all their energy into raising me. And they made sure to let me know how loved I was.' Which was the absolute truth, she realised with a sting of shame, because she'd distanced herself from them since leaving home in an attempt to leave her stultifying life there behind her. But she'd left them behind, too. They didn't deserve that. A visit was well overdue and she made a pact with herself to call them and arrange a date to see them as soon as she got back to London.

Max nodded, seemingly satisfied that she didn't need any more consoling, and broke eye contact to lean down and pick up another flat pebble.

She watched him weigh it in his palm, as if checking it was worth the effort of throwing it. Everything he did was measured and thorough like that, which was probably why he was such a successful businessman.

'Here, this looks like a good one. It's nice and flat with a decent weight to it so it'll fly and not sink immediately.' He turned it over in his hand. 'You need to get it to ride the air for a while before it comes down and maintain enough lift to jump.'

He held it out to her and she took it and looked at it with a frown. 'Is there a proper way to hold it?'

'I find the best way is to pinch it between my first finger and thumb. Like this.' He picked up another stone and demonstrated.

She copied the positioning in her own hand

then gave him a confident nod, drew back her arm and threw it as hard as she could.

It landed in the lake with a *plop* and sank immediately.

'Darn it! What did I do wrong?' she asked, annoyed with herself for failing so badly.

'Don't worry; it can take a bit of practice to get your technique right. You need to get lower to the ground and swing your arm in a horizontal arc. When it feels like the stone could fly straight forward and parallel with the water, loosen the grip with your thumb and let it roll, snapping your finger forwards hard.'

'Huh. You make it sound so easy.'

He grinned and raised his eyebrows. 'Try again.'

Picking up a good-looking candidate, she positioned the stone between her finger and thumb and was just about to throw it when Max said, 'Stop!'

Glancing round at him with a grimace of frustration, she saw he was frowning and shaking his head.

'You need to swing your arm at a lower angle. Like this.'

Before she could react, he'd moved to stand

directly behind her, putting his left hand on her hip and wrapping his right hand around the hand she was holding the stone in. Her heart nearly leapt out of her chest at the firmness of his touch and started hammering away, forcing the blood through her body at a much higher rate than was reasonable for such low-level exercise.

As he drew their arms backwards the movement made her shoulder press against the hard wall of his chest and she was mightily glad that he couldn't see her face at that precise moment. She was pretty sure it must look a real picture.

'Okay, on three we'll throw it together.' His mouth was so close to her ear she felt his breath tickle the downy little hairs on the outer whorl.

'One...two...three!'

They moved their linked hands in a sweeping arc, Cara feeling the power of Max's body push against her as the momentum of the move forced them forwards. She was so distracted by being engulfed in his arms she nearly didn't see the stone bounce a couple of times before it sank beneath the water.

'Woo-hoo!' Max shouted, releasing her to

take a step back and raise his hand, waiting for her to give him a high five.

The sudden loss of his touch left her feeling strangely light and disorientated—but now was not the time to go to pieces. Mentally pulling herself together, she swung her hand up to meet his, their palms slapping loudly as they connected, then bent down straight away, pretending to search the ground for another missile.

'Who taught you to skim stones? A brother?' she asked casually, grimacing at the quaver in her voice, before grabbing another good-looking pebble and righting herself.

He'd stooped to pick up his own stone and glanced round at her as he straightened up. 'No. I'm an only child. I think once my mother realised how much hard work it was raising me she was determined not to have any more kids.' He raised a disparaging eyebrow then turned away to fling the stone across the lake, managing five bounces this time. He nodded with satisfaction. 'I used to mountain bike over to a nearby reservoir with a friend from boarding school at the weekends and we'd have competitions to see who could get their stone the furthest,' he said, already searching the ground for another likely skimmer, his movements surprisingly lithe considering the size of his powerful body.

A sudden need to get this right overwhelmed her.

She wasn't usually a superstitious person, but she imagined she could sense the power in this one simple challenge. If she got this stone to bounce by herself, maybe, just maybe, everything would be okay.

She was throwing this for her pride and the return of her strength. To prove to Max—but mostly to herself—that she was resilient and capable and—dare she even suggest it?—brave enough to try something new, even if there was a good chance she'd fail spectacularly and end up looking foolish again.

Harnessing the power of positive thought, she drew back her hand, took a second to centre herself, then flung the stone hard across the water, snapping her finger like he'd taught her and holding her breath as she watched it sail through the air.

It dropped low about fifteen feet out and for a second she thought she'd messed it up, but her spirits soared as she saw it bounce twice before disappearing.

Spinning round to make a celebratory face at Max, she was gratified to see him nod in exaggerated approval, a smile playing about his lips.

'Good job! You're a quick study; but then we already knew that about you.'

The compliment made her insides flare with warmth and she let out a laugh of delight, elation twisting through her as she saw him grin back.

Their gazes snagged and held, his pupils dilating till his eyes looked nearly black in the bright afternoon light.

A wave of electric heat spread through her at the sight of it, but the laughter died in her throat as he turned abruptly away and stared off towards the house instead, folding his arms so tightly against his chest she could make out the shape of his muscles under his shirt.

He cleared his throat. 'You know, this place is just like the venue where Jemima and I got married,' he said, so casually she wondered how much emotion he'd had to rein in, in order to say it.

Ugh. What a selfish dolt she was. Here she'd been worrying about what he thought of her and her tales of woe, when he was doing battle with his own demons.

It had occurred to her earlier that morning, as she'd struggled to do up her dress, that attending a wedding could be problematic for him, but she'd forgotten all about it after the incident in the kitchen, her thoughts distracted by the unnerving tension that had crackled between them ever since.

Or what she'd thought was tension.

Perhaps it had been apprehension on his part.

And then, when he'd mentioned how transient and lonely his youth had been over drinks earlier, it had brought it home to her why Jemima's death had hit him so hard. It sounded as if she'd been the person anchoring his life after years of feeling adrift and insecure. And this place reminded him of everything he'd lost.

No wonder he seemed so unsettled.

He'd still come here to help her out, though, despite his discomfort at being at this kind of event, which was a decent and kind thing for him to do and way beyond the call of duty as her boss. Her heart did a slow flip in her chest as she realised exactly what it must have cost him to agree to come.

'I'm sorry for dragging you here today. I didn't think about how hard it would be for you. After losing Jemima.'

He put his hand on her arm and waited for her to look at him before speaking. 'You have nothing to apologise for. *Nothing*. I wanted to come here to support you because you've done nothing but support me for the last few weeks. It's my turn to look after you today.' He was looking directly at her now and the fierce intensity in his eyes made a delicious shiver zip down her spine.

'Honestly, I thought it would be awful coming here,' he said, casting his gaze back towards the house again, 'but it's not been the trial I thought it'd be. In fact—' he ran a hand over his hair and let out a low breath '—it's been good for me to confront a situation like this. I've been missing out on so much life since Jem died and it's time I pulled my head out of the sand and faced the world again.'

Cara swallowed hard, ensnared in the emotion of the moment, her heart thudding against her chest and her breath rasping in her dry throat. Looking at Max now, she realised that the ever-present frown was nowhere to be seen for once. Instead, there was light in his eyes and something else…

They stood, frozen in the moment, as the gentle spring wind wrapped around them and the birds sang enthusiastically above their heads.

It would be so easy to push up onto tiptoe and slide her hands around his neck. To press her lips against his and feel the heat and masculine strength of him, to slide her tongue into his mouth and taste him. She ached to feel his breath against her skin and his hands in her hair, her whole body tingling with the sensory expectation of it.

She wanted to be the one to remind him what living could be like, if only he'd let her.

To her disappointment, Max broke eye contact with her and nodded towards the marquee behind them. 'We should probably get back before they send out a search party. We don't want to find ourselves in trouble for messing with Amber's schedule of events and being frogmarched to our seats,' he said lightly, though his voice sounded gruffer than normal.

Had he seen it in her face? The longing.

She hoped not. The thought of her infatuation putting their fragile relationship under any more strain made her insides squirm.

Anyway, that tension-filled moment had probably been him thinking about Jemima again.

Not her.

They walked in silence back to the marquee, the bright sun pleasantly warm on the back of her neck and bare shoulders, but her insides icy cold.

Despite their little detour, they weren't the last to sit down. It was with a sigh of relief that Cara slumped into her seat and reached for the bottle of white wine on the table, more than ready to blot out the ache of disappointment that had been present ever since he'd suggested they give up their truancy from the festivities and head back into the fray.

It wasn't that she didn't want to be here exactly; it was just that it had been so much fun hanging out with him. Just the two of them together, like friends. Or something.

Knocking back half a glass of wine in one go, she refilled it before offering the bottle to Max.

He was looking at her with bemusement, one eyebrow raised. 'Thirsty?'

Heat flared across her cheeks. 'Just getting in the party mood,' she said, forcing a nonchalant smile. 'It looks like we have some catching up to do.'

The raucous chatter and laughter in the room suggested that people were already pretty tiddly on the cocktails they'd been served.

'Okay, well, I'm going to stick to water if I have to drive to the bed and breakfast place later. I think one of us should stay sober enough to find our way there at the end of the night. I don't fancy kipping in the car.'

She gave him an awkward grin as the thought of sleeping in such close proximity to him made more heat rush to her face.

Picking up her glass, she took another long sip of wine to cover her distress.

Oh, good grief. It was going to be a long night.

The meal was surprisingly tasty, considering how many people were being catered for, and Cara began to relax as the wine did its work. She quickly found herself in a conversation with the lady to her right, who turned out to be Amber's second cousin and an estate agent in Angel, about the dearth of affordable housing to rent in London. By the end of dessert, the woman had promised to give Cara first dibs on a lovely-sounding one-bedroom flat that was just about to come onto her books. And that proved to Cara, without a shadow of a doubt, that you just had to be in the right place at the right time to get lucky.

Turning to say this exact thing to Max, she was disturbed to find he'd finished his conversation with the man next to him and was frowning down at the tablecloth.

'Sorry for ignoring you,' she said, worried he was getting sucked down into dark thoughts again with all the celebrating going on around him.

He gave her a tense smile and pushed his chair away from the table. 'You weren't. I overheard your conversation about finding a flat; that's great news—you should definitely get her number and follow that up,' he said, standing and tapping the back of his chair. 'I'm going to find the bathrooms. I'll be back in a minute.'

She watched him stride away with a lump in her throat. Was he upset about the prospect of her moving out? She dismissed the notion immediately. No, he couldn't be. He must be craving his space again by now. Even though she'd loved living there, she knew it was time to move out. Especially now that her feelings for him had twisted themselves into something new. Something dangerous.

'That's a good one you've got there—very sexy,' Amber's second cousin muttered into her ear, pulling back to waggle her eyebrows suggestively, only making the lump in Cara's throat grow in size.

Unable to speak, she gave the woman what she hoped looked like a gracious smile.

'Hi, Cara.'

The voice behind her made her jump in her seat and she swivelled round, only to find herself staring into the eyes of the woman she'd been trying to avoid since spotting her in the church earlier.

Her meal rolled uncomfortably in her stomach.

'Hi, Lucy.'

Instead of the look of cool disdain Cara was expecting, she was surprised to see Lucy bite her lip, her expression wary.

'How are you?' Lucy asked falteringly, as if afraid to hear the answer.

'Fine, thank you.' Cara kept her voice deliberately neutral, just in case this was an opening gambit to get her to admit to something she really didn't want to say.

'Can I talk to you for a moment?'

Cara swallowed her anxiety and gestured towards the chair Max had vacated, wondering what on earth this woman could have to say to her. Whatever it was, it was better to get it over with now so she didn't spend the rest of the night looking over her shoulder. Straightening her back, she steeled herself to deal with anything she could throw at her.

Lucy sat on the edge of the seat, as close as she could get to Cara without touching her, and laid her hands on her lap before taking a deep breath. 'I wanted to come over and apologise as soon as I could so there wasn't any kind of atmosphere between us today.'

Cara stared at her. 'I'm sorry? Did you say *apologise*?'

Lucy crossed her legs, then uncrossed them again, her cheeks flooding with colour. 'Yes… I'm really sorry about the way you were treated at LED. I feel awful about it. I let Michelle bully me into taking her side—because I knew she'd turn on me, too, if I stood up for you—and I was pathetic enough to let her. I want you to know that I didn't do any of those awful things to you, but I didn't stop it either.' She shook her head and let out a low sigh. 'I feel awful about it, Cara, truly.'

At that moment Cara felt a pair of hands land lightly on her shoulders. Twisting her head round, she saw that Max had returned and was standing over her like some kind of dark guardian angel.

'Everything okay, Cara?' From the cool tone in his voice she suspected he'd be more than willing to step in and eject Lucy from her seat if she asked him to.

'Fine, thanks, Max. This is Lucy. She came over to apologise for her *unfriendliness* at the last place I worked.'

'Is that so?'

Cara couldn't see the expression on his face from that angle but, from the sound of his voice and the way Lucy seemed to shrink back in her chair, she guessed it wasn't a very friendly one.

Lucy cleared her throat awkwardly. 'Yes, I feel dreadful about the whole thing. It was horrible working there. In fact, I left the week after you did. I couldn't stand the smug look on Michelle's face any more. Although—' she leaned forward in a conspiratorial manner '—I heard from one of the other girls that she only lasted a month before he got rid of her. She couldn't hack it, apparently.' She snorted. 'That's karma in action, right there.' Clearly feeling she'd said her piece, Lucy stood up so that Max could have his chair back and took a small step away from them. 'Anyway, I'd better get back to my table; apparently there's coffee on the way and I'm desperate for some. Those cocktails were evil, weren't they?'

'Why are you here today?' Cara asked before she could turn and leave, intrigued by the coincidence.

'I'm Jack's—the groom's—new PA.'

Cara couldn't help but laugh at life's weird little twist. 'Really?'

'Yeah, he's a great boss, really lovely to work for.' She leant forward again and said in a quiet voice, 'I don't think Amber likes me very much, though; she didn't seem very pleased to see me here.'

'I wouldn't take that too personally,' Cara said, giving her a reassuring smile. 'She's an intensely protective person.' She put a hand on Lucy's arm. 'Thanks for being brave enough to come over and apologise, Lucy; I really appreciate the gesture.'

Lucy gave her one last smile, and Max a slightly terrified grimace, before retreating to her table.

Max sat back down in his chair, giving her an impressed nod. 'Nicely handled.'

Warm pleasure coursed through her as she took in the look of approval in his eyes. Feeling a little flustered by it, she picked up her glass of wine to take a big gulp, but judged the tilt badly and some escaped from the side of the rim and dribbled down her chin. Before she had time to react, Max whipped his napkin under her jaw and caught the rogue droplets with it, stopping them from splashing onto her dress.

'Smooth!' she said, laughing in surprise.

'I have moves,' he replied, his eyes twinkling and his mouth twitching into a warm smile.

A wave of heat engulfed her and her stomach did a full-on somersault.

Oh, no, what was *happening* to her?

Heart racing, she finally allowed the truth to filter through to her consciousness.

It was, of course, the very last thing she needed to happen.

She was falling in love with him.

CHAPTER EIGHT

AFTER THE MEAL and speeches, all the guests were encouraged to go through to the house, where a bar had been set up under the sweeping staircase in the hall and a DJ in the ballroom was playing ambient tunes in the hope of drawing the guests in there to sit around the tables that surrounded the dance floor.

Waiting at the bar to grab them both a caffeinated soft drink to give them some energy for the rest of the evening's events, Max allowed his thoughts to jump back over the day.

He'd had fun at the lake with Cara, which had taken him by surprise, because the last thing he'd expected when he'd got up that morning was that he would enjoy himself today.

But Cara had a way of finding the joy in things.

In fact, he'd been so caught up in the pleasure of showing her how to skim stones, he hadn't thought about what he was doing until his hand was on the soft curve of her hip and his body was pressed up close to hers, the familiar floral scent of her perfume in his nose and the heat of her warming his skin. He'd hidden his instinctive response to it well enough, he thought, using the excessive rush of adrenaline to hurl more stones across the water.

And then she'd been so delighted when she'd managed to skim that stone by herself he'd felt a mad urge to wrap his arms around her again in celebration and experience the moment with her.

But that time he'd managed to rein himself in, randomly talking about his own wedding to break the tension, only to feel a different kind of self-reproach when Cara assumed his indiscriminate jump to the subject was down to him feeling gloomy about his situation.

Which it really hadn't been.

Returning with the drinks to where he'd left Cara standing just inside the ballroom, he handed one to her and smiled when she received it with a grimace of relieved thanks. The main lights in the room were set low and a large glitter ball revolved slowly from the ceiling, scattering the floor and walls with shards of silver light. Max watched them dance over Cara's face in fascination, thinking that she looked like some kind of ethereal seraph, with her bright eyes and pale creamy skin against the glowing silver of her dress.

A strange elation twisted through him, triggering a lifting sensation throughout his whole body—as if all the things that had dragged him down in the past eighteen months were losing their weight and slowly drifting upwards. The sadness he'd expected to keep on hitting him throughout the day was still notably absent, and instead there was a weird sense of rightness about being here.

With her.

Catching her giving him a quizzical look, he was just about to ask if she wanted to take another walk outside so they could hear each other speak when Jack and Amber walked past them and onto the empty dance floor. Noticing their presence, the DJ cued up a new track as a surge of guests crowded into the room, evidently following the happy couple in to watch their first dance as husband and wife.

Max found himself jostled closer to Cara

as the edges of the dance floor filled up and he instinctively put an arm around her to stop her from being shoved around, too. She turned to look at him, the expression in her eyes startled at first, but then sparking with understanding when he nodded towards a gap in the crowd a little along from them.

He guided them towards it, feeling her hips sway against his as they moved, and had to will his attention-starved body not to respond.

Once in the space, he let her go, relaxing his arm to his side, and could have sworn he saw her shoulders drop a little as if she'd been holding herself rigid.

Feeling a little disconcerted by her obvious discomfort at him touching her again, he watched the happy couple blindly as they twirled around the dance floor, going through the motions of the ballroom dance they'd plainly been practising for the past few months.

Had he overstepped the mark by manhandling her like that? He'd not meant to make her uncomfortable but they were supposed to be there as a couple, so it wasn't as though it wasn't within his remit to act that way around her.

Ugh. There was no point in beating himself

up about it. He'd just have to be more careful about the way he touched her, or not, for the rest of the evening.

As soon as the dance finished, other couples joined the newlyweds on the dance floor and, spotting Cara, Jack broke away from Amber and made his way over to them.

'Cara, I'm so glad you made it!' he said, stooping down to pull her into a bear hug, making her squeal with laughter as he spun her around before placing her back down again.

Cara pulled away from him, her cheeks flushed, and rubbed his arm affectionately. 'Congratulations. And thank you for inviting us. It's a beautiful wedding.'

'I'm glad you're having a good time,' Jack replied, smiling into her eyes. 'Want to dance with me, for old times' sake?' he said, already taking her arm and leading her away from Max onto the dance floor. 'You don't mind if I steal her away for a minute, do you, Max?' he tossed over his shoulder, plainly not at all interested in Max's real opinion on the matter.

Not that Max *should* mind.

Watching Cara laugh at something that Jack whispered into her ear as he began to move her around the dance floor, Max was hit by an unreasonable surge of irritation and had to force himself to relax his arms and let them hang by his sides instead of balling them into tight fists. What the heck was going on with him today? How messed up was he to be jealous of a new groom, who was clearly infatuated with his wife, just because he was dancing with Cara? It must be because the guy seemed to have everything—a wife who loved him, a successful career with colleagues who respected him, Cara as a friend...

The track came to a close and a new, slower one started up. Before he could check himself, Max strode across to where Jack and Cara were just breaking apart.

'You don't mind if I cut in now, do you?' he said to Jack, intensely conscious that his words had come out as more of a statement than a question.

Jack's eyebrows rose infinitesimally at Max's less than gracious tone, but he smiled at Cara and swept a hand to encompass them both. 'Be my guest.' Leaning forward, he kissed Cara on the cheek before moving away from her. 'It's great to see you so happy. You

know, you're actually glowing.' He slapped
Max on the back. 'You're obviously good for
her, Max. Look after her, okay? She's a good
one,' he said. 'But watch your feet; she's a bit
of a toe-stamper,' he added, ducking out of
the way as Cara swiped a hand at him and
walked off laughing.

Turning back, Cara fixed Max with an
awkward smile, then leaned in to speak into
his ear. 'Sorry about that. I didn't want to
admit to the truth about us and break the
mood.'

Max nodded, his shoulders suddenly stiff,
surprised to find he was disappointed to hear
her say that her glow was nothing to do with
him.

*Don't be ridiculous, you fool—how could
it be?*

His feelings must have shown on his face
because she took a small step away from him
and said, 'You don't really need to dance with
me, but thanks for the gesture.'

He shrugged. 'It's no problem. You seemed
to be enjoying yourself and I was anticipating
Jack being commandeered at any second by
Amber or another relative wanting his attention so I thought I'd jump in,' he replied, feel-

ing the hairs that had escaped from her up-do tickle his nose as he leaned in close to her.

She looked at him for the longest moment, something flickering behind her eyes, before giving him a small nod and a smile. 'Okay then, I'd love to dance.'

Holding her as loosely as he could in his arms, he guided her around the dance floor, leading her in a basic waltz and finding pleasure in the way she responded to his lead, copying his movements with a real sense that she trusted him not to make a false step. His blood roared through his veins as his heart worked overtime to keep him cool in the accumulated heat of the bodies that surrounded them. Or was it the feeling of her in his arms that was doing that to him?

He felt her back shift against his palm and turned to see she was waving to Lucy, the woman who had come over to apologise to her at dinner.

A sense of admiration swept thorough him as he reflected on how well she'd handled that situation. When he'd returned to the table, after needing to take a breath of air and talk himself down from a strange feeling of despondency when he heard she was likely to find a new place to live soon, and seen them talking, he'd feared the worst. An intense urge to step in and protect her had grabbed him by the throat, making him move fast and put his hands on her, to let her know he had her back if she needed him.

She hadn't, though. In fact she'd shown real strength and finesse with her response. Another example of why she was so good at her job. And why he respected her so much as a person. Why he liked her—

Halting his thoughts right there, he guided her over to the side of the dance floor as the music changed into retro pop and drew away from her, feeling oddly bereft at the loss of her warm body so close to his own.

The room was spinning.

And it wasn't from the alcohol she'd consumed earlier or even the overwhelming heat and noise—it was because of Max. Being so close to him, feeling the strength of his will as he whirled her around the dance floor had sent her senses into a nosedive.

'Max, do you mind if we go outside for a minute? I need some air.'

The look her gave her was one of pure alarm. 'Are you all right?'

'I'm fine, just a bit hot,' she said, flapping a hand ineffectually in front of her face.

Giving her a curt nod, he motioned for her to walk out of the ballroom in front of him, shadowing her closely as she pushed her way through the crowd of people in the hallway and out into the blissfully cool evening air.

Slumping down onto a cold stone bench pushed up against the front of the house, she let out a deep sigh of relief as the fresh air pricked at her hot skin.

'I'm going to fetch you a drink of water,' Max said, standing over her, his face a picture of concern. 'Stay here.'

She watched him go, her stomach sinking with embarrassment, wondering how she was ever going to explain herself if she didn't manage to pull it together.

Putting her head in her hands, she breathed in the echo of Max's scent on her skin, its musky undertones making her heart trip over itself.

'Are you okay there?'

The deep voice made her start and she looked up to see one of the male guests looking down at her, his brow creased in worry. She seemed to remember Amber's second cousin pointing him out as Amber's youngest brother and the black sheep of the family. *Womaniser* was the word she'd used.

Sitting up straighter in her seat, she gave him a friendly but dispassionate smile. 'I'm fine, thanks, just a bit hot from dancing.'

Instead of nodding and walking away, he sat down next to her and held out his hand. 'I'm Frank, Amber's black sheep of a brother,' he said with a twinkle in his eye.

She couldn't help but laugh as she shook his hand. 'I'm Cara.'

'I don't know whether anyone's told you this today, Cara, but you look beautiful in that dress,' he said, his voice smooth like melted chocolate. He wanted her. She could see it in his face.

Cara was just about to open her mouth to politely brush him off when a shadow fell across them. Looking up, she saw that Max had returned with her glass of water and was standing over them with a strange look on his face.

'Here's your drink, Cara,' he said, handing it over and giving Frank a curt nod.

Frank must have seen something in Max's expression because he got up quickly and took a step away from them both. 'Okay, well, it looks like your boyfriend's got this, so I'll say good evening. Have a good one, Cara,' he said, flashing her a disappointed smile as he backed away, then turning on his heel to disappear into the dark garden.

'Sorry,' Max said gruffly, 'I didn't mean to scare him off.' He didn't look particularly sorry, though, she noted as he sat down next to her and laid his arm across the back of the bench. In fact, if anything, he seemed pleased that the guy had gone. Turning to look him directly in the eye, her stomach gave a flutter of nerves as something flickered in his eyes. Something fierce and disconcerting.

Telling herself she must be seeing things, she forced a composed smile onto her face. 'It's okay; he wasn't my type anyway.'

Not like you.

Pushing the rogue thought away, she took a long sip of the water he'd fetched to cover her nerves. What was she doing, letting herself imagine there was something developing between them?

'Thanks for the water. I didn't mean to

worry you. I'm feeling better now I'm in the fresh air.'

Despite her claims, he was still looking at her with that strange expression in his eyes.

'Why are you single?' he asked suddenly, making her blink at him in surprise.

'Oh, you know…'

He frowned. 'It's not because I've been working you too hard, is it?'

'No, no!' She shook her head. 'It's through personal choice.'

His frown deepened, as if he didn't quite believe her.

She swallowed before expanding on her answer, linking her fingers tightly together around the glass. 'I decided to take a break from dating for a while. My last relationship was a bit of a disaster.'

He relaxed back against the bench. 'How so?'

'The whole fiasco at LED pretty much ruined it. After I started having trouble coping with what was going on at work I got a bit down and it made me withdraw into myself. My ex-boyfriend, Ewan, got fed up with me being so…er…*unresponsive*.' She cringed. 'That's why I've been trying so hard to stay positive. I know how it can get boring, having people around who feel sorry for themselves all the time.'

He ran his hand through his hair, letting out a long, low sigh.

Heat rushed through her as she realised how Max might have interpreted what she'd just said. 'I didn't mean… I wasn't talking about you.'

He snorted gently and flashed her a smile. 'I didn't think you were. I was frustrated on your behalf. I can't believe the guy was stupid enough to treat you like that.'

'Yeah, well, it's in the past now. To be honest, that relationship was always doomed to fail. He was a little too self-centred for my liking. He made it pretty obvious he thought I wasn't good enough for him.'

'Not good enough! That's the most ridiculous thing I ever heard,' he snapped out, the ferocity in his tone telling her he had a lot more he wanted to say on the matter, but for the sake of propriety was keeping it to himself.

She smiled at him, her heart rising to her throat. 'It's okay. It doesn't bother me any more.' And it really didn't, she realised with a sense of satisfaction. Her experiences since breaking up with Ewan had taught her that her real self-worth came from her own actions and achievements, not pleasing someone else.

Putting the empty glass onto the ground by the bench, she tried to hide a yawn of tiredness behind her hand. It had been a long and intense day.

'Do you want to get out of here?' Max asked quietly.

Clearly she hadn't been able to hide her exhaustion from him.

Looking at him with a smile of gratitude, she nodded her head. 'I wouldn't mind. I don't think I've got the energy for any more dancing.'

He stood up. 'Okay, I'll go and fetch the car.'

'I'll just pop back in and say goodbye to Jack and Amber and I'll meet you back here,' she said, gesturing to the pull-in place at the end of the sweeping driveway.

He nodded, before turning on his heel and heading off towards where they'd left the car parked by the estate's church.

She watched him disappear into the darkness, with his jacket slung over his arm and the white shirt stretched across his broad shoulders glowing in the moonlight, before he dipped out of sight.

After saying a hurried goodbye to the now rather inebriated newlyweds, she came out to find Max waiting for her in the car and jumped in gratefully, sinking back into the soft leather seat with a sigh. Now she knew that bed wasn't far away, she was desperate to escape to her room and finally be able to relax away from Max's unsettling presence.

It only took them five minutes to drive to the B&B she'd booked them into and as luck would have it there was a convenient parking space right outside the pretty thatched cottage.

'We're in the annexe at the back,' she said to Max as he hauled their overnight bags out of the boot. 'They gave me a key code to open the door so we won't need to disturb them.'

'Great,' Max said, hoisting the bags onto his back and following her down the path of the colourful country cottage garden towards the rear of the house. The air smelled sweetly of the honeysuckle that wound itself around a large wooden arch leading through to the back garden where their accommodation was housed, and Cara breathed it in with a great sense of pleasure. The place felt almost magical, shrouded as it was in the velvety darkness of the night.

Cara tapped the code into the keypad next to the small oak door that led directly into the annexe and flipped on the lights as soon as they were inside, illuminating a beautifully presented hallway with its simple country-style furniture and heritage-coloured décor. Two open bedroom doors stood opposite each other and there was a small bathroom at the back, which they would share.

'I hope this is okay. All the local hotels were fully booked and Jack said this was the place his cousin and her family were going to stay in, so the owners were pleased to swap the booking to us, considering it was such a last-minute cancellation.'

Max nodded, looking around at the layout, his expression neutral. 'It's great.'

The hallway was so small they were standing much closer to each other than Cara was entirely comfortable with. Max moved past her to drop his bag into one of the rooms and his musky scent hit her senses, making her whole body quiver with longing. The thought of him being just a few feet away from her was going to make it very difficult to sleep, despite how tired she was.

After dropping her bag into the other room, Max walked back into the hallway and stood in front of her, a small frown playing across his face. 'Are you feeling okay now?'

She smiled, the effort making her cheeks ache. 'I'm fine.' She took a nervous step backwards, and jumped a little as her back hit the wall behind her. 'Thank you so much for coming with me. I really appreciate it.'

He was looking at her with that fierce expression in his eyes again and a heavy, tingly heat slid from her throat, deep into her belly, sending electric currents of need to every nerve-ending in her body. For some reason she was finding it hard to breathe.

'It was my pleasure, Cara,' he said, his voice gruff as if he was having trouble with his own airways. 'You know, that guy you were talking to earlier was right. You do look beautiful in that dress.'

She stared at him, a disorientating mixture of excitement and confusion swirling around her head.

His gaze flicked away from hers for a second and when his eyes returned to hers the fierce look had gone and was replaced with a friendly twinkle. 'It occurred to me that you might have a bit of trouble getting out it— after needing my help to do it up this morning. Want me to undo the buttons for you?'

What was this?

Cara knew what she wanted it to be: for Max to want the same thing that she did—to alleviate this unbearable need to touch and kiss and hold him. To slide off all their clothes and lose themselves in each other's body.

To love him.

Did he want that, too?

Could he?

Her heart was beating so hard and fast, all she could hear and feel was the hot pulse of her blood through her body.

'That would be great. Thank you,' she managed to force past her dry throat.

She rotated on the spot until her back was to him, her whole body vibrating with tension as she felt his fingers graze her skin as he released each of the buttons in turn.

As soon as the last one popped free, she trapped the now loose dress against her body and turned to face him again, trying to summon an expression that wouldn't give her feelings away.

He looked at her for the longest time, his eyes wide and dark and his breathing shallow.

She watched him flick his tongue between his lips and something snapped inside her. Unable to stand the tension any longer, she rocked forward on her toes and tipped her head up, pressing her mouth to his. His lips were firm under hers and his scent enveloped her, wrapping round her senses, only adding to her violent pull of need to deepen the kiss.

Until she realised he wasn't kissing her back.

He hadn't moved away from her, but she could feel how tense he was under her touch. As if he was holding himself rigid.

She stilled, one hand anchoring herself against his broad shoulder, the other still holding her dress tightly against her body, and pulled away, eyes screwed shut, her stomach plummeting to her shoes at his lack of response.

What had she *done*?

When she dared open her eyes, he was looking at her with such an expression of torment that she had to close them again.

'I'm sorry. So, so sorry,' she whispered, her throat locking up and her face burning with mortification.

'Cara—' He sounded troubled. Aggrieved. Exasperated.

Stumbling away from him, her back hit the wall again and she felt her way blindly into her bedroom and slammed the door shut, leaning back on it as if it would keep out the horror of the past few seconds.

Which, of course, it wouldn't.

What must he think of her? All he'd done was offer to help her with her dress and she'd thrown herself at him. What had possessed her to do that when she knew he wasn't over losing his wife? How could she have thought he wanted anything more to develop between them?

She was a fool.

And she couldn't even blame it on alcohol because she'd been drinking soft drinks for the past couple of hours.

She jumped in fright as she felt Max knock on the door, the vibration of it echoing through her tightly strung body. She knew she had to face him. To apologise and try to find some way to make things right again.

Struggling to get her breathing under control, she stepped away from the door and opened it, forcing herself to look up into Max's face with as much cool confidence as she could muster.

Before he could say anything, she held up a hand. 'I really am sorry… I don't know what happened. It won't ever happen ag—'

But, before she could finish the sentence, he took a step towards her, the expression in his eyes wild and intense as he slid his hand into her hair, drawing her forward and pressing his lips against hers.

They stumbled into the room, off balance, as their mouths crashed together. Electric heat exploded deep within her and she heard him groan with pleasure when she pressed her body hard into his. She could feel the urgency in him as he pushed her back against the wall, his hard body trapping her there as he fervently explored her mouth with his own, his tongue sliding firmly against hers. Taking a step back, he pulled his shirt over his head in one swift movement and dropped it onto the floor next to them.

'Are you sure you want this, Cara?' he asked, his voice guttural and low as she feverishly ran her hands over the dips and swells of his chest in dazed wonder.

'Yes.'

She smiled as he exhaled in relief and brought his mouth back down to hers, sliding his hands down to her thighs so he could pick her up and carry her over to the bed.

Then there was no more talking, just the feel of his solid body pressed hard against hers and the slide and twist of his muscles under his soft skin and—sensation—a riot of sensation that she sunk into and lost herself in. Her body had craved this for so long it was a sweet, beautiful relief to finally have what she wanted.

What she needed.

In those moments there was no past and no future; they were purely living for the moment.

And it was absolutely perfect.

CHAPTER NINE

MAX AWOKE FROM such a deep sleep it took him a while to realise that he wasn't in his own bed.

And that he wasn't alone.

Cara's warm body was pressed up against his back, her arm draped heavily over his hip and her head tucked in between his shoulder blades. He could feel her breath against his skin and hear her gentle exhalations.

Memories from the night they'd just spent together flitted through his head like a film on fast-forward, the intensity of them making his skin tingle and his blood pound through his body. It had been amazing. More than amazing. It had rocked his world.

It had felt so good holding her in his arms, feeling her respond so willingly to his demands and clearly enjoying making her own on him.

But, lying here now, he knew it had been a mistake.

It was too soon after losing his wife to be feeling like that. It felt wrong—somehow seedy and inappropriate. Greedy.

He'd had his shot at love and it wasn't right that he should get another one. Especially not so soon after losing Jemima. In the cold light of day it seemed tasteless somehow, as if he hadn't paid his dues.

He'd been in such a fog of need all day yesterday that he'd pushed all the rational arguments to the back of his head and just taken what he'd wanted, which had been totally unfair on Cara.

He wasn't ready to give himself over to a relationship again. And he knew that Cara would need more from him than he was able to give. She'd want the fairy tale, and he was no Prince Charming.

The worst thing was: he'd known that this was going to happen. From the moment he'd set eyes on her. He'd been attracted to her, even though he'd pretended to himself that he wasn't. And he'd only made things worse for himself by keeping her at arm's length. The more he'd told himself *no*, the more he'd wanted her. That was why he'd really thought it best to get rid of her quickly, before anything could happen between them. And then, once it became clear there was no hiding from the fact she was a positive force in his life, he'd pretended to himself that he wanted her to stay purely for her skills as a PA.

Idiot.

It had well and truly backfired on him.

This was precisely why he'd stopped himself from becoming friends with her at the beginning. He'd known it would guide them down a dangerous path.

His concerns hadn't stopped him from knocking on her door after she'd run away from him last night, though. Even after it had taken everything he'd had not to respond to that first kiss. But she'd looked so hurt, so devastatingly bereft that he'd found himself chasing after her to try and put it right. And, judging by her reaction when he'd been unable to hold back a second time and stop himself from kissing her, she'd been just as desperate as him for it to happen. In fact, the small, encouraging noises that had driven him wild made him think she'd wanted it for a while.

And, as his penance, he was now going to have to explain to her why it could never happen again.

Drawing away from her as gently as he could so as not to wake her, he swung his legs out of bed and sat on the edge, putting his head in his hands, trying to figure out what to do next. He wasn't going to just leave her here in the middle of rural Leicestershire with no transport, but the thought of having to sit through the whole car journey home with her after explaining why last night had been a mistake filled him with dread.

He jumped as a slender arm snaked round his middle and Cara kissed down the length of his spine, before pulling herself up to sit behind him with her legs on either side of his body, her breasts pressing into his back.

'Good morning,' she said, her voice guttural with sleep.

Fighting to keep his body from responding to her, he put his hand on the arm that was wrapped around his middle and gently prised it away.

'Are you okay?' she asked, her tone sounding worried now.

'Fine.' He stood up and grabbed his trousers, pulling them on roughly before turning back to her.

She'd tugged the sheet around her and was looking up at him with such an expression of concern he nearly reached for her.

Steeling himself against the impulse, he shoved his hands in his pockets and looked at her with as much cool determination as he could muster.

'This was wrong, Cara. Us, doing this.'

'What?' Her eyes widened in confused surprise.

'I'm sorry. I shouldn't have let it happen. I got caught up in the moment, which was selfish of me.'

Her expression changed in an instant to one of panic. 'No.' She held out her hands beseechingly. 'Please don't be sorry about it. I wanted it to happen, too.'

He swallowed hard, tearing his eyes away from her worried gaze. 'I can't give you what you want long-term, Cara.'

Pulling the sheet tighter around her body, she frowned at him. 'You don't know what I want.'

He smiled sadly. 'Yes, I do. You want this

to turn into something serious, but I don't. I'm happy with my life the way it is.'

'You're *happy*?' She looked incredulous.

He rubbed his hand over his face in irritation. 'Yes, Cara, I'm happy,' he said, but he felt the lie land heavily in his gut.

'But what we had last night—and all day yesterday—I didn't imagine it.' She shook her head as if trying to throw off any niggling doubts. 'It was so good. It felt right between us, Max. Surely you felt that, too.'

He looked at her steadily, already hating himself for what he was about to say. 'No. Sorry.' He scrubbed a hand through his hair. 'Look, I was feeling lonely and you happened to be there. I feel awful about it and I won't blame you for being angry.'

She didn't believe him; he could see it in her eyes.

'I understand why you're panicking,' she said, holding out her hands in a pleading gesture, 'because we've just changed the nature of our relationship and it's a scary thing, taking things a step further, especially after what happened to Jemima…'

'See, that's the thing, Cara. I've been through

that once and I'm not prepared to put myself through something like that again.'

'But it was so random—'

'The type of illness isn't the point here. It's the idea of pouring all your love into one person, only to lose them in the blink of an eye. I can go through that again.'

'But you can't cut yourself off from the world, Max. It'll drive you insane.'

He took a pace forward and folded his arms across his chest. 'You want to know what really drives me insane—that my wife was lying there in hospital with the life draining out of her and there wasn't a thing I could do about it. Not one damn thing. I promised her I'd look after her through thick and thin. I failed, Cara.' His throat felt tight with emotion he didn't want to feel any more.

'You didn't fail.'

He rubbed a hand over his eyes, taking a deep breath to loosen off the tension in his chest. 'I'm a fixer, Cara, but I couldn't fix that.'

'There wasn't anything you could have done.'

'I could have paid her more attention.'

'I'm sure she knew how much you loved her.'

And there was the rub. He did love Jemima. Too much to have room for anyone else in his heart.

'Yes, I think she did. But that doesn't change anything between you and me. I don't want this, Cara,' he said, waggling a finger between the two of them.

She stared at him in disbelief. 'So that's it? You've made up your mind and there's nothing I can do to change it?'

'Yes.'

Tipping up her chin, she looked him dead in the eye. 'Do you still want me to work for you?' she asked, her voice breaking with emotion.

Did he? His working life had been a lot less stressful since she'd been around, but what had just happened between them would make his personal life a lot more complicated. They were between a rock and a hard place. 'Yes. But I'll understand if it's too uncomfortable for you to stay.'

'So you'd let me just walk away?'

He sighed. 'If that's what you want.'

The look she gave him chilled him to the bone. 'You know, I don't believe for a second that Jemima would have wanted you to mourn her for the rest of your life. I think she'd have wanted you to be happy. You need to stop hiding behind her death and face the world again. Like you said you were going to yesterday. What happened to that, Max? Hmm? What happened to *you*? Jemima might not be alive any more, but *you* are and you need to stop punishing yourself for that and start living again.'

'I'm not ready—'

'You know, I love you, Max,' she broke in loudly, her eyes shining with tears.

He took a sharp intake of breath as the words cut through him. No. He didn't want to hear that from her right now. She was trying to emotionally manipulate him into doing something he didn't want to do.

'How can you love me?' Anger made his voice shake. 'We barely know each other.'

'I know you, Max,' she said calmly, her voice rich with emotion.

'You might think you do because I've told you a few personal things about myself recently, but that doesn't mean you get who I am and what I want.'

'Do you know what you want? Because it seems to me you're stopping yourself from being happy on purpose. You enjoyed being with me yesterday, Max, I know it.'

'I did enjoy it, but not in the way you think. It was good to get out of the house and have some fun, but that's all it was, Cara, *fun*.'

She shook her head, her body visibly shaking now. 'I don't believe you.'

'Fine. Don't believe me. Keep living in your perfect little imaginary world where everything is jolly and works out for the best, but don't expect me to show up.'

She reacted as if his words had physically hurt her, jolting back and hugging her arms around herself. 'How can you say that to me?'

Guilt wrapped around him and squeezed hard. She was right; it was a low blow after what he'd already put her through, but he was being cruel to be kind. Sinking onto the edge of the bed, he held up a pacifying hand. 'You see, I'm messed up, Cara. It's too soon for me. I'm not ready for another serious relationship. Maybe I'll never be ready. And it's not fair to ask you to wait for me.'

Her shoulders stiffened, as if she was fighting to keep them from slumping. 'Okay. If that's the way you feel,' she clipped out.

'It is, Cara. I'm sorry.'

The look she gave him was one of such disappointed disdain he recoiled a little.

'Well, then, I guess it's time for me to leave.' She shuffled to the edge of the bed. 'I'm not going to stick around here and let you treat me like I mean nothing to you. I'm worth more than that, Max, and if you can't appreciate that, then that's your loss.' With the sheet still wrapped firmly around her, she stood up and faced him, her eyes dark with anger. 'You can give me a lift to the nearest train station and I'll make my own way back to London.' Turning away from him, she walked over to where her overnight bag sat on the floor.

'Cara, don't be ridiculous—' he started to say, his tone sounding so insincere he cringed inwardly.

Swivelling on the spot, she pointed a shaking finger at him. 'Don't you dare say I'm the one being ridiculous. I'm catching the train. Please go and get changed in your own room. I'll meet you by the car in fifteen minutes.'

'Cara—' He tried to protest, moving towards her, but it was useless. He had nothing left to say.

There was no way to make this better.

'Okay,' he said quietly.

He watched her grab her wash kit from her bag, his gut twisting with unease.

Turning back, she gave him a jerky nod and then, staring resolutely ahead, went to stride past him to the bathroom.

Acting on pure impulse, he put out a hand to stop her, wrapping his fingers around her arm to prevent her from going any further. He could feel her shaking under his grip and he rubbed her arm gently, trying to imbue how sorry he was through the power of his touch.

She put her hand over his and for a second he thought she was going to squeeze his hand with understanding, but instead she pulled his fingers away from her arm and, without giving him another look, walked away.

Cara waited until Max's car had pulled away from the train station before sinking onto the bench next to the ticket office and putting her head in her hands, finally letting the tears stream down her face.

She'd spent the whole car journey there—which had only taken about ten minutes but had felt like ten painful hours—holding her head high and fighting back the hot pressure in her throat and behind her eyes.

They hadn't uttered one word to each other since he'd started the engine and she was grateful for that, because she knew if she'd had to speak there was no way she'd be able to hold it together.

It seemed they'd come full circle, with him withdrawing so far into himself he might as well have been a machine and her not wanting to show him any weakness.

What a mess.

And she'd told him she loved him.

Her chest cramped hard at the memory. When the words left her mouth, she hadn't known what sort of reaction to expect; in fact she hadn't even known she was going to say them until they'd rolled off her tongue, but she was still shocked by the flare of anger she'd seen in his eyes.

He'd thought she was trying to manipulate him, when that had been the last thing on her mind at the time. She'd wanted him to know he was loved and there could be a future for them if he wanted it.

Thinking about it now, though, she realised she had been trying to shock him into action. To reach something deep inside him that he'd been fiercely protecting ever since Jemima had died. It wasn't surprising he'd reacted the way he had, though. She couldn't begin to imagine the pain of losing a spouse, but she understood the pain of losing someone you loved in the blink of an eye or, in this case, in the time it took to say three small words.

Fury and frustration swirled in her gut, her empty stomach on the edge of nausea. How could she have let herself fall for a man who was still grieving for his wife and had no space left in his heart for her?

Clearly she was a glutton for punishment. And, because of that, she'd now not only lost her heart, she'd lost her home and her job, as well.

Back in London three hours later, she let herself wearily into Max's house, her nerves prickling at the thought of him being there.

Part of her wanted to see him—some mad voice in the back of her head had been whispering about him changing his mind after having time to reflect on what she'd said—but the other, sane part told her she was being naïve.

Walking into the kitchen, she saw that a note had been left in the middle of the table with her name written on it in Max's neat handwriting.

Picking it up with a trembling hand, she read the words, her stomach twisting with pain and her sight blurring with tears as she took in the news that he'd gone to Ireland a couple of days early for his meeting there, to give them a bit of space.

He wasn't interested in giving them another chance.

It was over.

Slumping into the nearest chair, she willed herself not to cry again. There was no point; she wasn't going to solve anything by sitting here feeling sorry for herself.

She had to look after herself now.

Her life had no foundations any more; it was listing at a dangerous angle and at some point in the near future it could crash to the ground if she didn't do something drastic to shore it up.

She'd *so* wanted to belong here with him, but this house wasn't her home and Max wasn't her husband.

His heart belonged to someone else.

She hated the fact she was jealous of a ghost, and not just because Jemima had been beautiful and talented, but because Max loved her with a fierceness she could barely comprehend.

How could she ever compete with that?

The stone-cold truth was: she couldn't.

And she couldn't stay here a moment longer either.

After carefully folding her clothes into her suitcase, she phoned Sarah to ask whether she could sleep on her couch again, just until she'd moved into the flat that Amber's cousin had promised to let to her.

'Sure, you'd be welcome to stay with us again,' Sarah said, after finally coaxing out the reason for her needing a place to escape to so soon after moving into Max's house. 'But you might want to try Anna. She's going to be away in the States for a couple of weeks from tomorrow and I bet she'd love you to housesit for her.'

One phone call to their friend Anna later and she had a new place to live for the next couple of weeks. So that was her accommodation sorted. Now it was just the small matter of finding a new job.

She'd received an email last week from one of the firms that she'd sent a job application to, offering her an interview, but hadn't had time to respond to it, being so busy keeping the business afloat while Max was in Manchester. After firing off an email accepting an interview for the Tuesday of that week, she turned her thoughts to her current job.

Even though she was angry and upset with Max, there was no way she was just going to abandon the business without finding someone to take over the role she'd carved out for herself. Max might not want her around, but he was still going to need a PA. The meeting he had with a large corporation in Ireland later this week was an exciting prospect and if he managed to land their business he was going to need to hire more staff, pronto.

So this week it looked as if she was going to be both interviewer and interviewee.

The thought of it both exhausted and saddened her.

But she'd made her bed when she'd shared hers with Max, and now she was going to have to lie in it.

CHAPTER TEN

MAX HAD THOUGHT he was okay with the decision to walk away from a relationship with Cara, but his subconscious seemed to have other ideas when he woke up in a cold sweat for the third day running after dreaming that Cara was locked in the house whilst it burnt to the ground and he couldn't find any way to get her out.

Even after he'd been up for a while and looked through his emails, he still couldn't get rid of the haunting image of Cara's face contorted with terror as the flames licked around her. Despite the rational part of his brain telling him it wasn't real, he couldn't shake the feeling that he'd failed her.

Because, of course, he had, he finally accepted, as he sat down to eat his breakfast in the hotel restaurant before his meeting. She'd laid herself bare for him, both figuratively and literally, and he'd abused her trust by treating her as if she meant nothing to him.

Which wasn't the case at all.

He sighed and rubbed a hand over his tired eyes. The last thing he should be doing right now was worrying about how he'd treated Cara when he was about to walk into one of the biggest corporations in Ireland and convince them to give him their business. This was exactly what he'd feared would happen when he'd first agreed to let her work for him—that the business might suffer. Though, to be fair to Cara, this mess was of his own making.

Feeling his phone vibrate, he lifted it out of his pocket and tapped on the icon to open his text messages. It was from Cara.

With his pulse thumping hard in his throat, he read what she'd written. It simply said:

Good luck today. I'll be thinking of you.

A heavy pressure built in his chest as he read the words through for a second time.

She was thinking about him.

Those few simple words undid something in him and a wave of pure anguish crashed through his body, stealing his breath and making his vision blur. Despite how he'd treated her, she was still looking out for him.

She wanted him to know that he wasn't alone.

That was so like Cara. She was such a good person: selfless and kind, but also brave and honourable. Jemima would have loved her.

Taking a deep breath, he mentally pulled himself together. Now was not the time to lose the plot. He had some serious business to attend to and he wasn't about to let all the work that he and Cara had put into making this opportunity happen go to waste.

Fourteen hours later Max flopped onto his hotel bed, totally exhausted after spending the whole day selling himself to the prospective clients, then taking them out for a celebratory dinner to mark their partnership when they signed on the dotted line to buy his company's services.

He'd done it; he'd closed the deal—and a very profitable deal it was, too—which meant he could now comfortably grow the business and hire a team of people to work for him.

His life was moving on.

A strong urge to call Cara and let her know he'd been successful had him sitting up and reaching for his phone, but he stopped himself from tapping on her name at the last second. He couldn't call her this late at night without it *meaning* something.

Frustration rattled through him, swiftly followed by such an intense wave of despondency it took his breath away. He needed to talk to someone. Right now.

Scrolling through his contacts, he found the name he wanted and pressed *call*, his hands twitching with impatience as he listened to the long drones of the dialling tone.

'Max? Is everything okay?' said a sleepy voice on the other end of the line.

'Hi, Poppy, sorry—I forgot it'd be so late where you are,' he lied.

'No problem,' his friend replied, her voice strained as if she was struggling to sit up in bed. 'What's up? Is everything okay?'

'Yes. Fine. Everything's fine. I won a pivotal contract for the business today so I'm really happy,' he said, acutely aware of how flat his voice sounded despite his best efforts to sound upbeat.

Apparently it didn't fool Poppy either. 'You

don't *sound* really happy, Max. Are you sure there isn't something else bothering you?'

His friend was too astute for her own good. But then she'd seen him at his lowest after Jemima died and had taken many a late night call from him throughout that dark time. He hadn't called her in a while though, so it wasn't entirely surprising that she thought something was wrong now.

'Er—' He ran a hand through his hair and sighed, feeling exhaustion drag at him. 'No, I'm—' But he couldn't say it. He wasn't fine. In fact he was far from it.

A blast of rage came out of nowhere and he gripped his phone hard, fighting for control.

It was a losing battle.

'You did it on purpose, didn't you? Sent Cara to me so I'd fall in love with her,' he said angrily, blood pumping hard through his body, and he leapt up from the bed and started to pace the room.

His heart gave an extra hard thump as the stunned silence at the other end of the line penetrated through his anger, bringing home to him exactly what he'd just said.

'Are you in love with her?' Poppy asked quietly, as if not wanting to break the spell.

He slapped the wall hard, feeling a sick satisfaction at the sting of pain in the palm of his hand. 'Jemima's only been dead for a year and a half.'

'That has nothing to do with it, and it wasn't what I asked you.'

He sighed and slumped back down onto the bed, battling to deal with the disorientating mass of emotions swirling though his head. 'I don't know, Poppy,' he said finally. 'I don't know.'

'If you don't know, that probably means that you are but you're too pig-headed to admit it to yourself.'

He couldn't help but laugh. His friend knew him so well.

'Is she in love with you?' Poppy asked.

'She says she is.'

He could almost feel his friend smiling on the other end of the phone.

Damn her.

'Look, I've got to go,' he said, 'I've had a very long day and my flight back to London leaves at six o'clock in the morning,' he finished, not wanting to protract this uncomfortable conversation any longer. 'I'll call you tomorrow after I've had some sleep and got my head straight, okay?'

'Okay.' There was a pause. 'You deserve to be happy though, Max, you know that, don't you? It's what Jemima would have wanted.'

He cut the call and threw the phone onto the bed, staring sightlessly at the blank wall in front of him.

Did he deserve to be happy, after the way he'd acted? Was he worthy of a second chance?

There was only one person who could answer that question.

The house was quiet when he arrived home at eight-thirty the next morning. Eerily so.

Cara should have been up by now, having breakfast and getting ready for the day—if she was there.

His stomach sank with dread as he considered the possibility that she wasn't. That she'd taken him at his word and walked away. Not that he could blame her.

Racing up the stairs, he came to an abrupt halt in front of her open bedroom door and peered inside. It was immaculate. And empty. As if she'd never been there.

Uncomfortable heat swamped him as he

made his way slowly back down to the kitchen. Perhaps she hadn't gone. Perhaps she'd had a tidying spree in her room, then gone out early to grab some breakfast or something.

But he knew that none of these guesses were right when he spotted her keys to the house and the company mobile he'd given her to use for all their communications sitting in the middle of the kitchen table.

The silence of the house seemed to press in on him, crushing his chest, and he slumped onto the nearest chair and put his head in his hands.

This was all wrong. *All* of it.

He didn't want to stay in this house any longer; it was like living in a tomb. Or a shrine. Whatever it was, it felt wrong for him to be here now. Memories of the life he'd had here with Jemima were holding him back, preventing him from moving on and finding happiness again. Deep down, he knew Jem wouldn't have wanted that for him. He certainly wouldn't have wanted her to mourn him for the rest of her life.

She'd want him to be happy.

Like he had been on Sunday night.

He was in love with Cara.

Groaning loudly into his hands, he shook his head, unable to believe what a total idiot he'd been.

Memories of Cara flashed through his mind: her generous smile and kind gestures. Her standing up to him when it mattered to her most. Telling him she loved him.

His heart swelled with emotion, sending his blood coursing through his body and making it sing in his ears.

So this was living. How he'd missed it.

A loud ring on the doorbell made him jump.

Cara.

It had to be Cara, arriving promptly at nine o'clock for work like she always did.

Please, let it be her.

Tension tightened his muscles as he paced towards the door and flung it open, ready to say what he needed to say to her now. To be honest with her. To let her know how much he loved her and wanted her in his life.

'Max Firebrace?'

Instead of Cara standing on his doorstep, there was a tall, red-haired woman in a suit giving him a broad smile.

'Yes. Who are you?' he said impatiently,

not wanting to deal with anything but his need to speak to Cara right then.

She held out a hand. 'I'm Donna, your new PA.'

The air seemed to freeze around him. *'What?'*

The smile she gave him was one of tolerant fortitude. 'Cara said you might be surprised to see me because you've been in Ireland all week.'

'Cara sent you here?'

'Yes, she interviewed me yesterday and said I should start today.'

He stared at her, stunned. 'Where is Cara?'

Donna looked confused. 'Er... I don't know. I wasn't expecting her to be here. She said something about starting a new job for a firm in the City next week. We spent all of yesterday afternoon getting me up to speed with the things I need to do to fulfil the role and went through the systems you use here, so I assumed she'd already served her notice.'

So that was it then. He was too late to save the situation. She was gone.

'You'd better come in,' he muttered, frustration tugging hard at his insides.

'So will we be working here the whole

time? It's a beautiful house,' Donna said brightly, looking around the hall.

'No. I'm going to rent an office soon,' he said distractedly, his voice rough with panic.

How was he going to find her? He didn't have any contact details for her friends or her personal mobile number; she'd always used the company one to call or text him. He could try Poppy, but she'd probably be out filming in the middle of the desert right now and wouldn't want to be disturbed with phone calls.

A thought suddenly occurred to him. 'Donna? Did Cara interview you here?'

'No. I went to her flat.' She frowned. 'Although, come to think of it, I don't think it was her place; she didn't know which cupboard the sugar for my drink was kept in.'

He paced towards her, startling her with a rather manic smile.

'Okay, Donna. Your first job as my PA is to give me the address where you met Cara.'

At first Cara thought that the loud banging was part of her dream, but she started awake as the noise thundered through the flat again, seeming to shake the walls. Whoever was knocking really wanted to get her attention.

Pulling her big towelling dressing gown on over her sleep shorts and vest top, she stumbled to the door, still half-asleep. Perhaps the postman had a delivery for one of the other flats and they weren't in to receive it.

But it wasn't the postman.

It was Max.

Her vision tilted as she stumbled against the door in surprise and she hung on to the handle for dear life in an attempt to stop herself from falling towards him.

'Max! How did you find me?' she croaked, her voice completely useless in the face of his shocking presence.

She'd told herself that giving them both some space to breathe was the best thing she could do. After leaving his house on Monday she'd tried to push him out of her mind in an attempt to get through the dark, lonely days without him, but always, in the back of her mind, was the hope that he'd think about what she'd said and maybe, at some point in the future, want to look her up again.

But she hadn't expected it to happen so soon.

'My new PA, Donna, gave me the address,'

he said, raising an eyebrow in chastisement, though the sparkle in his eyes told her he wasn't seriously angry with her for going ahead and hiring someone to take her place without his approval.

Telling herself not to get too excited in case he was only popping round to drop off something she'd accidentally left at the house, she motioned for him to come inside and led him through to the kitchen diner, turning to lean against the counter for support.

'You did say you'd understand if I couldn't work with you any more. After what happened,' she said.

He came to a stop a few feet away from her and propped himself against the table. 'I did.'

She took a breath and tipped up her chin. 'I'm not made of stone, Max. As much as I'd like to sweep what happened on Sunday under the carpet, I can't do that. I'm sorry.'

Letting out a long sigh, he shifted against the table. 'Don't be sorry. It wasn't your fault. It was mine. I was the one who knocked on your door when you had the strength to walk away.'

She snorted gently. 'That wasn't strength; it was cowardice.'

'You're not a coward, Cara; you just have a strong sense of self-preservation. You should consider it a gift.'

She stared down at the floor, aware of the heat of her humiliation rising to her face, not wanting him to see how weak and out of control she was right now.

'So you start a new job next week?' he asked quietly.

Forcing herself to look at him again, she gave him the most assertive smile she could muster. 'Yes, at a place in the City. It's a good company and the people were very friendly when they showed me around.'

'I bet you could handle just about anything after having to work for me.' He smiled, but she couldn't return it this time. The muscles in her face wouldn't move. They seemed to be frozen in place.

Gosh, this was awkward.

'You've been good for my confidence.' She flapped a hand at him and added, 'Work-wise,' when he raised his eyebrows in dispute. 'You were great at letting me know when I'd done a good job.'

'Only because you were brave enough to point out how bad I was at it.'

She managed a smile this time, albeit a rather wonky one. 'Well, whatever. I really appreciated it.'

There was a tense silence where they both looked away, as if psyching themselves up to tackle the real issues.

'Look, I'm not here to ask you to come back and work for me again,' Max said finally, running a hand over his hair.

'Oh. Okay,' she whispered, fighting back the tears. She would not break down in front of him. She *wouldn't*.

He frowned, as if worried about the way she'd reacted, and sighed loudly. 'Argh! I'm so bad at this.' He moved towards her but stopped a couple of feet away, holding up his hands. 'I wanted to tell you that I think I've finally made peace with what happened to Jemima. Despite my best efforts to remain a reclusive, twisted misery guts, I think I'm going to be okay now.' He took another step towards her, giving her a tentative smile. 'Thanks to you.'

Forcing down the lump in her throat, she smiled back. 'That's good to hear, Max. Really good. I'm happy that you're happy. And I do understand why you don't want me to come back and work for you. It must have been hard having me hanging around your house so much.'

'I'm going to sell the house, Cara.'

She stared at him in shock, her heart racing. 'What? But—how can you stand to leave it? That beautiful house.'

'I don't care about the house. I care about us.' This time he walked right up to her, so close she could feel the heat radiating from his body, and looked her directly in the eye. 'I'm ready to live again and I want to do it with you.'

'You—?'

'Want *you*, Cara.' His voice shook with emotion and she could see now that he was trembling.

'But—? I thought you said—when did you…?' Her voice petered out as her brain shut down in shock.

He half smiled, half frowned. 'Clearly I need to explain some things.' He took her hand and led her gently over to the sofa in the living area, guiding her to sit down next to him, keeping his fingers tightly locked with hers and capturing her gaze before speaking.

'When we slept together I felt like I'd betrayed a promise to Jemima.' He swallowed hard. 'After what happened to her I thought I had no right to be happy and start again when she couldn't do that. I truly thought I'd never love someone else the way I loved her, but then I realised I didn't need to. The love I feel for you is different—just as strong, but a different flavour. Does that make sense?'

He waited for her to nod shakily before continuing. 'I don't want to replicate Jemima or the way it was with her. I want to experience it all afresh with you. I'll always love Jem because she was a big part of my life for many years, but I can compartmentalise that now as part of my past.' He squeezed her fingers hard. 'You're my future.'

'Really?' Her throat was so tense with emotion she could hardly form the word.

'Yes. I love you, Cara.'

And she knew from the look on his face that he meant every word. He'd never given up anything of an emotional nature lightly and she understood what a superhuman effort it must have taken for him to come here and say all that to her.

Reaching out a hand, she ran her fingers

across his cheek, desperate to smooth away any fears he might have. 'I love you, too.'

He closed his eyes and breathed out hard in relief before opening them again, looking more at peace than she'd ever seen him before. Lifting his own hand, he slid his fingers into her hair and drew her towards him, pressing his mouth to hers and kissing her long and hard.

She felt it right down to her toes.

Drawing away for a moment, he touched his forehead to hers and whispered, 'You make me so happy.'

And then, once again, there was no more talking. Just passion and joy and excitement for their bright new future together.

EPILOGUE

One year later

THE HOUSE THEY'D chosen to buy together was just the sort of place Cara had dreamed of owning during her romantic but practical twenties. It wasn't as grand or impressive as the house in South Kensington, but it felt exactly right for the two of them. And perhaps for any future family that chose to come along.

Not that having children was on the cards *right* now. Max was focusing hard on maintaining the expansion of his Management Solutions business, which had been flying ever since the Irish company awarded him their contract, and Cara was happy in her new position as Executive Assistant to the CEO of the company she'd joined in the City. But they'd talked about the possibility of it happening in the near future and had both agreed it was something they wanted.

Life was good. And so was their relationship.

After worrying for the first few months that, despite his assurances to the contrary, Max might still be in the grip of grief and that they had some struggles ahead of them, her fears had been assuaged as their partnership flourished and grew into something so strong and authentic she could barely breathe with happiness some days.

Max's anger had faded but his fierceness remained, which she now experienced as both a protective and supportive force in her life. Being a party to his sad past had taught her to count her blessings, and she did. Every single day.

Arriving home late after enjoying a quick Friday night drink with her colleagues, she let herself into their golden-bricked Victorian town house—which they'd chosen for the views of Victoria Park and its close location to the thriving bustle and buzz of Columbia Road with its weekly flower market and kitschy independent furniture shops—and stopped dead in the doorway, staring down at the floor.

It was covered in flowers, of all colours and varieties. Frowning at them in bewilderment, she realised they were arranged into the shape of a sweeping arrow pointing towards the living room.

'Max? I'm home. What's going on? It looks like spring has exploded in our hallway!'

Tiptoeing carefully over the flowers so as not to crush too many of them, she made her way towards the living room and peered nervously through the doorway, her heart skittering at the mystery of it.

What she saw inside took her breath away.

Every surface was covered in vibrantly coloured bouquets of spring flowers, displayed in all manner of receptacles: from antique vases to the measuring jug she used to make her porridge in the mornings. Even the light fitting had a large cutting of honeysuckle spiralling down from it, its sweet fragrance permeating the air. It reminded her of their first night together after Jack's wedding. Which quickly led her to memories of all the wonderful nights that had come after it, where she'd lain in Max's arms, breathing in the scent of his skin, barely able to believe how loved and cherished she felt.

And she was loved, as Max constantly reminded her, and her support and love for him had enabled him to finally say goodbye to Jemima and the past that had kept him ensnared for so long.

She'd unlocked his heart.

She was the key, he'd told her as he carried her, giggling, over the threshold into their house six months ago.

She'd finally found her home.

Their home.

He was standing next to the rose-strewn piano in the bay, looking at her with the same expression of fierce love and desire that always made her blood rush with heat.

'Hello, beautiful, did you have a good night?' he asked, walking towards where she stood, his smile bringing a mesmerising twinkle to his eyes.

'I did, thank you.' She swept a hand around the room, unable to stop herself from blurting, 'Max, what is this?'

The reverent expression on his face made her heart leap into her throat. 'This is me asking you to marry me,' he said, dropping to one knee in front of her and taking her hand in his, smiling at her gasp of surprise.

'This time last year I thought I'd never want to be married again—that I didn't deserve to be happy—but meeting you changed all that. You saved me, Cara.' Reaching into his pocket, he withdrew a small black velvet-covered box and flipped it open to reveal a beautiful flower-shaped diamond ring.

'I love you, and I want to spend the rest of my life loving you.' His eyes were alive with passion and hope. 'So what do you say—will you marry me?'

Heart pounding and her whole body shaking with excitement, she dropped onto her knees in front of him and gazed into his face, hardly able to believe the intensity of the love she felt for him.

'Yes,' she said simply, smiling into his eyes, letting him know how much she loved him back. 'Yes. I will.'

* * * * *

LARGER-PRINT BOOKS!
GET 2 FREE LARGER-PRINT NOVELS PLUS
2 FREE GIFTS!

HARLEQUIN®
Romance

From the Heart, For the Heart

YES! Please send me 2 FREE LARGER-PRINT Harlequin® Romance novels and my 2 FREE gifts (gifts are worth about $10). After receiving them, if I don't wish to receive any more books, I can return the shipping statement marked "cancel." If I don't cancel, I will receive 4 brand-new novels every month and be billed just $5.09 per book in the U.S. or $5.49 per book in Canada. That's a savings of at least 15% off the cover price! It's quite a bargain! Shipping and handling is just 50¢ per book in the U.S. and 75¢ per book in Canada.* I understand that accepting the 2 free books and gifts places me under no obligation to buy anything. I can always return a shipment and cancel at any time. Even if I never buy another book, the two free books and gifts are mine to keep forever.

119/319 HDN GHWC

Name	(PLEASE PRINT)	
Address		Apt. #
City	State/Prov.	Zip/Postal Code

Signature (if under 18, a parent or guardian must sign)

Mail to the **Reader Service:**
IN U.S.A.: P.O. Box 1867, Buffalo, NY 14240-1867
IN CANADA: P.O. Box 609, Fort Erie, Ontario L2A 5X3
Want to try two free books from another line?
Call 1-800-873-8635 or visit www.ReaderService.com.

* Terms and prices subject to change without notice. Prices do not include applicable taxes. Sales tax applicable in N.Y. Canadian residents will be charged applicable taxes. Offer not valid in Quebec. This offer is limited to one order per household. Not valid for current subscribers to Harlequin Romance Larger-Print books. All orders subject to credit approval. Credit or debit balances in a customer's account(s) may be offset by any other outstanding balance owed by or to the customer. Please allow 4 to 6 weeks for delivery. Offer available while quantities last.

Your Privacy—The Reader Service is committed to protecting your privacy. Our Privacy Policy is available online at www.ReaderService.com or upon request from the Reader Service.

We make a portion of our mailing list available to reputable third parties that offer products we believe may interest you. If you prefer that we not exchange your name with third parties, or if you wish to clarify or modify your communication preferences, please visit us at www.ReaderService.com/consumerschoice or write to us at Reader Service Preference Service, P.O. Box 9062, Buffalo, NY 14240-9062. Include your complete name and address.

Dom walked past the double sofas, over to the bar, and when he turned to pour his Scotch, he saw the door to Ginny's suite door was open. And there she stood. A short man wearing spectacles and a white shirt with the sleeves rolled to his elbows had a tape measure around her hips. Her mom stood with her back to the door, obviously supervising.

Dom stared. He'd forgotten how perfect she was.

The short dark-haired guy raised the tape measure to her waist and Dom followed every movement of the man's hands, remembering the smoothness of her shape, the silkiness of her skin. The tailor whipped the tape around and snapped the two ends together in the middle, right above her belly button, and Dominic's head tilted.

Right there…

Right below that perfect belly button…

Was his child.

His child.

His hand went limp and the glass he was holding fell to the bar with a thump.

Ginny's head snapped up and she turned to see him standing there, staring. Their eyes met. And it hit him for the very first time, not that she was pregnant, but that the baby she carried was *his*.

His baby.

Don't miss
PREGNANT WITH A ROYAL BABY!
by Susan Meier,
available February 2016 wherever
Harlequin® Romance books and ebooks are sold.

www.Harlequin.com